What did readers think of the first book in this series,

Tales from the Deed Box of John H. Watson MD?

"…delicately woven stories in the Conan Doyle tradition so that the reader cannot decipher where Conan Doyle's brilliant sleuth leaves off and where Ashton's begins. Truly a masterful addition to the Holmes legacy of wit, sleuthing and surprises!"
Linda Rae Blair

"These are marvelous stories where all elements including descriptions of settings, characters and plot are done to perfection. The author has followed the approaches of the original Doyle stories to the extent that these could have been easily included in the original works."
Dr Darold C Simms

"As a life long Sherlock Holmes fan, I can say I truly enjoyed these three new stories. Hugh Ashton does a great job in the tradition of Sir Arthur Conan Doyle."
Vince Drexelius

"Mr. Ashton's offering of three stories, two of which are mentioned in passing by Dr. Watson in his well beloved chronicling of their adventures, are so faithful to the characters in these wonderful stories, it almost seems that Doyle himself has been resurrected."
M C McColl

More From the Deed Box of John H. Watson MD

Further Untold Tales of
Sherlock Holmes

As Discovered By
Hugh Ashton

More from the Deed Box of John H. Watson MD
Hugh Ashton

ISBN-13: 978-1470194840

ISBN-10: 1470194848

Published by Inknbeans Press, 2012

© 2012 Hugh Ashton and Inknbeans Press

All rights reserved. Without limiting the rights under copyright reserved above, no part of this publication may be reproduced, stored in or introduced into a retrieval system, or transmitted, in any form, or by any means (electronic, mechanical, photocopying, recording, or otherwise) without the prior written permission of both the copyright owner and the above publisher of this book.

This is a work of fiction. Names, characters, places, brands, media, and incidents are either the product of the author's imagination or are written in respectful tribute to the creator of the principal characters.

www.inknbeans.com

www.221BeanBakerStreet.info

Inknbeans Press, 1251 Sepulveda Blvd., Suite 475, Torrance, CA 90502, USA

Book design and cover by j-views

Body in Adobe Caslon Pro, titles in Garamond Premier

Contents

Dedications VI
Preface. VII
The Case of Colonel Warburton's Madness 11
The Mystery of The Paradol Chamber 81
The Giant Rat of Sumatra 155
About the Author 220

DEDICATIONS

ANY THANKS to all who have assisted in making this latest collection of stories available in their present form:

To all those at Inknbeans Press, and Jo, the Boss Bean, for their sharp eyes and ears, helping to smooth out the roughnesses and the infelicities of my writing.

To my readers, who, even in the short time that the first volume of my Holmes stories has been available, have turned it into a bestseller in its genre. I hope these tales will likewise meet with your approval.

And to Yoshiko, my patient wife, who has once again had to contend with the vicissitudes that accompany being married to an author.

Preface

Once again I am privileged to present to the world three tales of Sherlock Holmes that have long been locked in the deed box marked with the words "JOHN H. WATSON MD". This box had been stored in the vaults of a London bank for nearly a century before I took possession of the box.

Written in the distinctive and almost illegible handwriting of Dr Watson, these shed new light on this most famous of detectives. In several previously described cases, Holmes is content to let the suspect's own conscience, rather than the full rigour of the law, be the punishment for the crime – if the offence be not altogether serious. Indeed, in one of the cases recounted here, he goes further – not only allowing and assisting the perpetrator to escape punishment at the hands of the judicial system, but encouraging the official arm of the law, in the shape of Inspector Tobias Gregson, to aid and abet this escape. No wonder that *The Mystery of the Paradol Chamber* has remained untold for so long – such an action would hardly have rebounded to the credit of the Inspector.

Nor do these tales fail to shed light on the character of John H. Watson MD, late of the Indian Army. Far from being the passive observer and mere reflector of Holmes' brilliance that some have made him out to be (and as he himself at times deprecatingly refers to his role), he comes to life in these pages as a courageous man. His bravery as recounted in one of these tales, *The Giant Rat of Sumatra*, in attending a sick man, dying of a little-understood and usually fatal disease, cannot be denied; and he appears as one who, through a mixture of his own ability and the experience he had gained from working alongside Holmes, was himself no mean practitioner of the detective arts. Indeed, the more I read of Watson's writing, the more I come to wish that I had known him as a companion. And Holmes, to his credit, recognises Watson's worth on a number of occasions.

Each of the tales I have selected to recount here was mentioned by Watson in previous adventures, but only in passing, and the sketchy references have long been a source of curious speculation by students of the work of Sherlock Holmes.

The Case of Colonel Warburton's Madness is one of the few cases recorded by Watson as being one that he introduced to Holmes (*The Engineer's Thumb* being the other). Taking place in a seemingly innocuous suburban setting, it is nonetheless a tale of dark secrets and hidden evil. Holmes' skill at disguise is never seen to better advantage. Watson himself likewise shines as an investigator of more than average competence.

The Mystery of the Paradol Chamber is strangely named, and the mystery itself is a strange one where Holmes' talents are needed to unravel a classic "locked room" murder puzzle. Religion plays a very minor role in most of the cases described by Watson – it is interesting to see here that Holmes claims to have memorised the churches and incumbents of all the Roman Catholic (at least) churches in the English Home Counties.

Finally, the definitive story of *The Giant Rat of Sumatra*

has come to light. There are obvious reasons why this story was withheld from the public for so long. Even with the pseudonyms that have been so obviously employed, this story could have shaken the respectable world of English politics to the core if released. The cooperation of the Royal Navy with Holmes in the solving of this bizarre mystery is another aspect that would also have been kept secret, possibly at the behest of Mycroft.

These latest tales that I have unearthed will, I am confident, provide both enjoyment and instruction to all those who study and cherish the work of Sherlock Holmes. I hope to provide even more such tales, following further exploration of the contents of the deed box.

Hugh Ashton
Kamakura, 2012

Sherlock Holmes & The Case of Colonel Warburton's Madness

EDITOR'S NOTES

In The Engineer's Thumb, *Dr Watson refers to one other case that he introduced to Sherlock Holmes, that of Colonel Warburton's madness. This tale is one of those stored in the deed box, and we can only assume that Watson failed to include it in the published stories out of a sense of modesty. In this tale Watson exhibits many of the traits of the great detective, examining evidence and coming to conclusions independently of Holmes. Indeed, Holmes' opinion of Watson's value as an assistant is unequivocally stated here, and this tale, if no other, should give the lie to the idea that Watson was merely the dull foil to Holmes' rapier-like intelligence.*

My friend, the consulting detective Sherlock Holmes, was typically the recipient of direct requests for advice and help, which he provided according to his whims and fancies, usually dependent upon his opinion of whether the case was of sufficient interest to challenge his abilities. On more than one occasion, however, I was the cause of introducing him to a problem. One of these, an account of which I have already given in "The Case of the Engineer's Thumb", was of considerable interest to the authorities, concerning as it did a group of counterfeiters who were undermining the trust that the public places in the currency of this realm. The other case, though of considerable interest to a detective, was of far less concern to the public interest, and concerned Colonel Warburton, the former commander of the regiment in which I had served in my time in India.

The combination of my practice and my marriage had for some time deprived me of the company of Sherlock Holmes, and it appeared that I was settling into a domestic routine which was far removed from the days when he and I had tracked the malefactors of London and brought them to justice. I was more than content with my marriage to Mary, which indeed had brought me all the happiness that I had foreseen when I made my original proposal to her. My practice too, although routine, nonetheless presented enough interest for me to be content with my lot, and not to hanker after the days of excitement in the past.

Since retiring from Army life, I had lost contact with most of my former comrades, so it was with a sense of surprise that I recognised Philip Purcell, whom I had known in Afghanistan as a young captain, when he walked into my consulting room. His complaint was minor – a chill brought on by the sudden change of climate – and I swiftly prescribed him the appropriate medicines before we fell to chatting of old times.

"I would have thought that you would have stayed in the service," said he. "We all imagined that that old 'Death or Glory' Watson was bound for a destiny greater than that of a mere general practitioner, if you will forgive my saying so."

I was flattered by this reminder of my old Army sobriquet – as who could not fail to be? – but explained that the wound I had received from an Afghan bullet had made it more difficult than I had at first imagined for me to keep up with the physical demands of army life. "In any case," I went on, "it has been my great good fortune to encounter, and if I may say so, to have the friendship of one of the great men of the age, Mr Sherlock Holmes."

"I have heard of the fellow," said Purcell. "I must say, though, that the accounts I have read make him sound like some kind of fraudster or trickster. Of course, one must always make allowances for the exaggeration of the journalist wallahs and the fellows who put about those stories regarding such people. It would hardly surprise me to learn that the stories are for the most part exaggerations, if not outright fabrications."

Notwithstanding our old acquaintance, I spoke with some heat. "You do my friend an injustice," I exclaimed. "And, if I may be so bold as to say so, you also do me an injustice. Were it not for my attempts to chronicle the adventures in which he has been involved, I venture to suggest that the name of Sherlock Holmes would be unknown to the public. He does not seek notoriety or fame – in many cases, he has given credit to the police where by far the greater part of the work in the case has been his. I can assure you in all sincerity that the accounts you have read of his exploits are nothing more nor less than the truth."

Purcell had the good grace to look somewhat abashed and to stammer an apology. "I confess that I had never associated the sawbones whom I knew out East with the 'John Watson' who was describing Sherlock Holmes. Believe me, my dear fellow, I had no wish to cast doubts on your veracity, or the ability of your friend. Indeed, if he is as remarkable as your accounts make him out to be, I might even wish to consult him on a matter close to me. The problem is, if I may speak totally frankly to you about this, that I am short of money right now, and I am not convinced I could afford the fees that I am sure he charges for his services."

I laughed. "You do not know Sherlock Holmes," I replied, still smiling. "I will not say that he displays a complete indifference to money, but it is of less importance to him than you might perhaps imagine. I have known many cases on which he has worked for their own sake, with no thought of reward, and some which he has taken on for prominent clients where he has received remuneration which might be considered exorbitant, considering the effort involved. If your case is of interest to him, you might well expect him to take it up purely as presenting a challenge to his deductive abilities."

My friend appeared relieved. "That is good to hear. And I take it that he is discreet in his enquiries, and does not publicise matters that are best kept hidden?"

I reassured him on that score. "If you would care to tell me, in complete confidence of course, of the general nature of the problem, it may be that I can give you some indications as to how Sherlock Holmes will approach your case. Indeed," I added, not without a touch of pride, "it may be that some of the methods that he has imparted to me in the course of our partnership, if I may term it so, could be applied by me in order to assist you."

"The matter concerns Alice Warburton. Maybe you remember her?"

"Indeed I do. You refer to the daughter of the former Colonel of our regiment, do you not?"

"The same. I love her, Watson," he exclaimed. "I love her more than life itself, and if that sounds extravagant, believe me I feel it to be true in my innermost heart."

"She cannot be more than a child," I protested.

"You have been away from the Army for too long," he smiled. "Maybe she was a mere child when you left us, but she is now a young woman, 23 years of age."

"She was a remarkably beautiful child, I recall."

"She has matured into the most beautiful of women," he replied. "Not only beautiful in her appearance, but she has the most pure mind imaginable. I am convinced also that she loves me in return."

I recognised the symptoms of infatuation, not having been immune to the malady myself in the past. Even so, I forbore from smiling, and proceeded to question him further. "I do not think from what you have told me so far, that you require the services of Sherlock Holmes merely to ensure the success of the upcoming nuptials. There must be some problem preventing the successful completion of your wooing, or you would not be considering the employment of a consulting detective."

"I am sorry to say that you are correct." He sighed deeply, and his head hung on his breast. "Now that I come to consider it, it may be that a doctor such as yourself will be more use than your friend." He paused, and I waited for his next words. "It may not be not so much that there is a problem with Alice herself, as with her father."

"The Colonel?"

"That is so. He has given many signs recently when I visited their house that all is not well up here." He tapped the side of his head significantly.

I was conscious that I was aping many of the mannerisms of my friend, but I sat back in my chair and placed my fingertips together while half closing my eyes. "Can you be a little more precise as to the symptoms?" I asked Purcell.

"I have been visiting the house for about a year now," he replied. "I go there perhaps once or twice in a month, and I stay for one or two nights each time as a guest of the family. For the most part, Colonel Warburton could not be kinder to me than if I was already married to Alice, and his hospitality leaves me in no doubt that I am an approved suitor for her hand. However, commencing about two months ago, there seemed to be a strange change in the Colonel's behaviour." He paused briefly, and I encouraged him to go on. "As it happens, Watson, I feel much less restraint in describing these peculiar happenings to you than I would to anyone else, given that you are both an old acquaintance of mine and a medical man."

"You intrigue me," I replied. "Pray continue."

"You must understand," my friend said to me, "that the Colonel's wife, that is to say, Alice's mother, passed away some years ago, just before the Colonel's return from India, and the household is accordingly a small one, consisting of the Colonel himself, Alice and two or three servants who live in. They live very quietly in a secluded villa just outside Guildford. I first observed the onset of the Colonel's strange behaviour one morning at breakfast. Alice was suffering from a headache and had elected to remain in her room, so only the Colonel and myself were partaking of the meal. Imagine my surprise, when in the middle of his conversation, the Colonel suddenly broke off in mid-sentence, seizing the boiled egg that he had just started to eat, opened the window, and flung the egg out of the window into the garden with an expression of fury. I was astounded, the more so because he quietly closed the window and returned to the table all smiles, continuing the conversation as if nothing untoward had occurred."

"Most singular," I observed. "This was about two months ago, you say?" making a note in my memorandum book.

"That is correct, and since then his behaviour seems to have become more and more extreme. Indeed, I fear for his sanity, and hence for the future sanity of my beloved Alice. Though I adore her, I cannot conceive of marriage to someone whose mental state is potentially so precarious. Tell me, Watson," and he leaned forward and almost whispered the next words in a confidential tone, "in your experience as a medical man, is insanity of this kind hereditary?"

"I hardly consider myself to be an expert in such matters," I replied. "It does appear, however, that disturbances of this kind are often passed from generation to generation. But you have only described one such instance, which might be a trifling matter attendant on some temporary inconvenience. For example, the egg may not have been boiled to his liking and he was suffering, maybe, from the effects of over-indulgence on the previous evening? I agree with you, however, that his reaction does seem extreme."

"If that were all," replied my friend, "I would not be so concerned, but events of a similar bizarre nature have continued to occur since then. For example, only three weeks ago while I was staying at the house, an event occurred that almost caused me to quit the spot immediately. Indeed, now that I come to reflect on it, I am amazed that I remained as a guest there."

"Pray continue."

"You should understand that the household retires to bed at an early hour – at about 10 o'clock. This is much earlier than my usual time for bed, and accordingly I usually remain awake in my room for several hours, reading, or otherwise occupying my time until I fall asleep. No doubt you, as a fellow old campaigner, pursue similar habits. In any event, it must have been about midnight, and I was wide awake, when I heard an extraordinary noise outside my bed-room door. It sounded like a kind of irregular shuffling, as if someone were dancing or skipping. Naturally, I opened the door and looked out. Imagine my surprise, not to mention my horror, when I beheld the Colonel in his night attire, positively skipping up and down the corridor with a fixed grin on his face. The smile was not one of pleasure, but appeared to me to be that of a maniac. I confess, Watson, I was completely at a loss as to what to do. I had heard something of the strength possessed by lunatics, among whose number I had now no choice but to regard the Colonel, and since I was the only able-bodied man in the house, it did not seem wise to me to involve myself in a physical struggle with him."

"Was he aware that you were observing him?" I asked.

"Most certainly he was. His eyes were actually fixed on mine while he was performing these extraordinary movements. For about a minute, I suppose, I was mesmerised by the sight, and I was unable to move from the spot. Eventually, I was able to tear myself away from the horrid spectacle and returned to my room, where I locked the door. I must admit that I was actually worried for the safety of the others in the house, not to mention my own, and I seriously considered raising the alarm and attempting to apprehend and restrain the Colonel. Again, given that I was the only man in the house, this course of action did not seem a wise one to me. I cast around the room for some object I could use as a weapon in self-defence should the Colonel decide to enter the room and attack me."

"You believed that to be a genuine possibility, then?"

"At the time I did. I was also, as you can readily imagine, afraid for Alice. I stood by the locked door, poker in hand, listening to the strange shuffling sounds as the Colonel continued his exertions. At length, the sounds ceased, and I unlocked my door and stepped out. The Colonel was walking along the corridor back to his own room, seemingly unaware of my presence. Suddenly he appeared to notice me and he turned.

"'Hallo,' he said to me. 'What on earth are you doing with that in your hand?', pointing to the poker that I was gripping. 'Come to that, young man, what are you doing out of bed at this time of night?' You may well believe that there was no answer that I could give him, especially considering that his face showed absolutely no trace of the exertion that his actions of only a few minutes before must have caused him. I stammered out some reply of having heard a noise that I believed might have been burglars, upon which he patted me on the shoulder in the most friendly fashion and wished me a good night."

"Is there more?"

"I am sorry to say that there is. Though the incident of the egg has yet to be repeated, the nocturnal skipping has occurred, to the best of my knowledge, at least twice more."

"To the best of your knowledge? You cannot be sure?"

"I felt after the previous occasion that it would not be wise to confront the Colonel while he was in one of these states of mind. Even so, I can positively assert that I have heard the noise of the skipping twice more – both times at midnight."

I pondered this for a few seconds. "And that is all?"

He sighed. "I would that it were all that I had to say in this regard, but there is more. Yesterday afternoon, I was staying at the Colonel's house. Alice had gone up to Town on some feminine errand, it was the parlour-maid's afternoon off, and the cook had gone to the local shops to order the provisions for that evening's meal. The Colonel and I were alone in the house, and I proposed to write some letters – I am a deucedly poor correspondent, so I felt that this would be an excellent opportunity for me to make amends. The Colonel, for his part, announced that he would take a nap after luncheon, as is his usual habit. I had finished the first letter and had barely started the second, when I heard a noise from the garden, and the sound somehow reminded me of the parade-ground. I may add that the room I occupy while I am a guest there overlooks their garden. Looking out of the window, I observed the Colonel, carrying a broomstick as though it were a rifle, barking out parade-ground drill commands and executing them himself – with some skill, I have to admit. Naturally, I found this disturbing, particularly given the fatuous smile on his face, which gave him an appearance of crude vacancy, a rather different expression from the one which I had observed during his skipping exercises. This last was more maniacal in nature, while on this occasion, the smile had more of idiocy to it. The parade-ground performance must have lasted for somewhere in the region of ten minutes, when the front doorbell rang. I remembered that the servants were absent, and was prepared to let the door go unanswered, lest the caller discover the Colonel in his present condition, when the Colonel himself appeared to hear the sound, and his whole demeanour changed. The rifle on his shoulder reverted to being a broomstick once more, and the vacancy on his face vanished, to be replaced by the usual alert look of intelligence that I am sure you remember well."

"Extraordinary!" I exclaimed.

"I watched him hurry into the house, and heard the sound of the front door being opened, and the caller admitted. In a minute or so, I heard the Colonel's voice bidding me descend to meet the caller, Chelmy."

"Why would the Colonel desire you to meet this person?" I inquired.

"Maybe I should have explained to you earlier that this Guy Chelmy is a friend of the family. He has always, as far as I can judge, lived in the area, and is therefore a neighbour of the Colonel. Some time ago, I gather, he was of assistance to the Colonel in some matters concerning his financial affairs – I do not know the details, and I have never asked for them – in such a way that he acquired and has retained the friendship of the Colonel, and also of Alice. He is in some ways a pleasant enough fellow, if a little strange at times, but is a frequent visitor to the Warburtons and appears to be always welcome there. He and I generally get along well enough, and often play a frame or two of billiards together, at which I confess I almost always lose. He is a player of considerable skill, whatever else he may be."

"Would you regard him as your rival for Alice's hand?"

Purcell laughed, somewhat unpleasantly. "Hardly a rival, old man. If you had seen the chap, you would not bother asking that question. He is a little shrimp of a fellow. He must be about fifty years old, and looks every minute of it. Without wishing to boast, Watson, I think that if you were laying odds on the matter, I would be an odds-on favourite, and he would be an outsider."

It pained me a little to hear him talk of the state of holy matrimony as if it were a horse race, but determined to hold my peace on that score.

"But there is more," he continued. "I love Alice, and as

I told you, I am sure – nay, I am certain – that she loves me. Yet just two days ago, I asked her to marry me."

"And her response?"

"She told me that she loves me with all her heart, but that she could not marry me. These were her very words on the subject, 'I cannot marry you'. That, and no more."

"You fear that she likewise doubts the mental stability of her father, and wishes to dissuade you from marriage?"

"It is the only conclusion open to me," he replied. "There was no hint of unfriendliness towards me at the time or afterwards. Her refusal, I am convinced, is not the result of anything I am or that I have done."

"To summarise what you have told me, then." I said, "you have observed Colonel Warburton behaving oddly on at least one occasion, and you fear this behaviour may be the symptom of some kind of derangement. This derangement you fear to be hereditary, and you therefore have concerns – valid ones, I would say at this stage, judging by your account – about marriage to his daughter. His daughter shares these concerns, and has therefore refused your offer of marriage. Does that form an adequate account of the facts?"

"It would seem to be so. Do you suppose your friend Mr Holmes will take the case?"

"I can but ask him," I replied. "Let me have an address where I can reach you, and I will let you know the answer in a few days."

Purcell's visit reminded me that I had not called upon Sherlock Holmes in some weeks, and I determined to remedy this omission. Accordingly, the following day saw me mounting the well-known staircase at 221B Baker Street to the rooms formerly shared by Holmes and myself, and now occupied solely by the detective. Mrs Hudson had given me to understand that Holmes was in residence, but had added that he was "very busy these days".

I was confident, however, that Holmes would welcome my interruption, and my confidence was not misplaced. Holmes opened the door in answer to my knock, and waved me wordlessly to my accustomed armchair.

"Have the goodness, Watson, not to speak a word for a few minutes while I work out the details of this case," he said, but there was that in his face that bespoke some sort of pleasure at the prospect of my company which belied the seeming coldness of his tone.

I silently took my place. After about ten minutes, Holmes made a request of me to verify a biographical detail in "Who's Who", without even deigning to glance in my direction. From any other person, I would have taken this as the height of rudeness, but in the case of Sherlock Holmes I accepted it as a matter of trust in my ability, and I was glad that he continued to regard my assistance to be of value to him in his work.

At length he ceased making notes in his book, and sat back.

"If you would pass me the Persian slipper upon the mantel, I would be grateful." I reached up and handed him the article in question, which was the accustomed, if decidedly eccentric, receptacle for his tobacco. He thanked me and filled his pipe with the coarse shag that he affected, before regarding me quizzically.

"I am delighted for your sake to see that both your marriage and your practice are flourishing," he remarked on an off-hand manner. "Though I must confess to a selfish side of me that regrets the loss of my Watson as a confidant and aide."

"How do you know these things?" I asked.

"Come, Watson, these are simple matters. Your hat and boots are immaculately maintained, as are all your garments. They are in much better condition, if I may say so, than when you and I shared these rooms. I am sure you have not yet attained the luxury of a personal valet, hence I conclude your wife is ensuring that you are turned out in such splendid style. This, to me, argues a happy marriage."

"I follow you so far. What of the medical practice?"

"Though your garments are cared for splendidly, they are not in a condition that suggests you sit and wait idly for custom to present itself to you. They bespeak a man of active habits, and given your profession, that would seem to argue a successful practice. There are, of course, other little pointers, such as the stains of iodine on your fingers where you have no injury, and the tell-tale bulge in your hat where you secrete your stethoscope, as I have remarked previously."

I laughed. "I must agree with you on both points regarding my happiness, and congratulate you once again on your perspicacity."

"Quite so, quite so," he replied, and busied himself in lighting his pipe. "And you are here to consult me on some matter on behalf of a friend?"

"Since I obviously have no troubles of my own, you mean?" I laughed. "Naturally, you are correct."

"Naturally," he repeated, with a slight smile.

I explained the position of my friend Purcell. During my recounting of the facts, Holmes said nothing, but gazed out of the window, while puffing at his pipe. To those who did not know him, it would appear that he was uninterested in my account, but I knew from experience that he was often at his most attentive under such circumstances. At length I concluded the tale of Colonel Warburton.

"An excellent summary, Watson. You have a gift on these occasions for presenting the necessary information in an order that makes it easy for me to examine the facts. Would that you exercised the same restraint when chronicling my cases for the benefit of the public," he sighed. "This Colonel Warburton was also your commanding officer in India? How would you characterise him?"

"A fair man, well-liked by those he commanded. He had a gift for keeping the regiment contented."

"Any weaknesses that you observed?" asked Holmes sharply.

"Other than the fact that he drank to excess at times, which was a fault to which the whole regiment, indeed, the whole of the Army at that time in that place, was prone, there is little, except perhaps a fondness for cards."

"Did he play for high stakes?"

"I was not in those circles," I replied, a little stiffly. "I never heard so, in any event."

"And the daughter?" asked Holmes.

"She was a mere girl when I left India. She was extraordinarily beautiful as a child, and the pet of the regiment. Other than that, I really cannot furnish any information."

"And your friend Purcell?"

"A somewhat impetuous young man when I knew him. He seems to have settled down a little since then, but I confess that he was more than a little disrespectful when it came to the subject of marriage."

"And your opinion of Colonel Warburton's madness, if we may term it thus?"

"'Madness' may be too strong a term. It is certainly eccentric, to say the least."

"It is very odd," agreed Holmes. "There are several very queer points about it, to me as a layman in these matters, at least."

"Will you help Purcell?" I asked.

"I will be delighted to give the matter my attention in a few days," he replied. "At the minute, I am engaged in a rather delicate case which involves the Earl of Lincoln and his gamekeeper. Although the case itself is simple, the matter of keeping it confidential is not. After a few days, I am hopeful that I will be able to turn to something more interesting."

"You consider this interesting, then?"

"Indeed I do. I am of the opinion that there is much more to this case than either you or your friend believe."

"And as for—"

"Ah, the question of money? I think your friend need lose no sleep on that score. This promises to be one of those cases that brings its own reward."

I refrained from asking questions. The problem, which at first sight had appeared to be one that had a solution that could be easily determined, seemed to Holmes to have depths unsuspected by me.

"Can your practice and your wife spare you for a few days?" he inquired of me.

"I can always hand over my practice to Jackson for two or three days, and Mary is able to take care of herself for the same period. Why do you ask?"

"I am wondering whether you can manage to renew your acquaintance with Colonel Warburton, and arrange to have yourself invited as a guest for a short period, preferably together with Purcell. Regular reports of your observations, addressed to me here at Baker Street, would be most valuable. If you can start today, so much the better."

"That could probably be arranged without too much difficulty. And what of you?"

"I will make my own plans, and you will be made aware of them, never fear," he replied.

On leaving Baker Street, I hailed a cab and made my way to the address Purcell had given me – a lodging-house in Bloomsbury. He greeted me in the parlour used by the lodgers, and listened to what I had to say.

"I must thank you for this," he said, when I had explained the outcome of my conversation with Holmes. "I feel we can send a wire to the old chap letting him know you are coming and travel down to Guildford without waiting for an answer. He's a perfectly decent old buffer, when he is not suffering from these queer fits. And I remember once how you pulled him through a bout of dysentery when he'd almost given himself up for lost. He'll be delighted to see you again, Doctor, and you would surely like to renew his acquaintance?" He spoke with the animation I have observed to be common to those of less ripe years when contemplating the meeting of old colleagues.

"Maybe under slightly strained circumstances," I gently reminded him, "after what you have described to me."

"Quite so, but let us send that telegram, and we can be on our way. I feel that I can speak for the Colonel when I say that you will be welcome in his house."

Nor, in the event, was Purcell's confidence in Colonel Warburton's hospitality misplaced. Having been forewarned of my arrival by the telegram we had dispatched prior to our departure, his welcome was as warm as one could wish for. As he shook my hand with every evidence of friendship, I scanned his face as unobtrusively as possible for signs of the illness that Purcell had described, but was unable to discern any trace of abnormality in his features. He remained a fine figure of a man, tall and powerfully built, and still carried himself with a military bearing. It was not hard to imagine his past as a successful and popular leader of men.

On entering the drawing-room, we were greeted by

Alice Warburton, who was acting as our hostess. As Purcell had told me, she had matured into an extraordinarily beautiful young woman, with china-blue eyes set in a face framed by golden hair. I was hardly surprised that Purcell was so strongly attracted to her, based on her appearance, but her conversation seemed to me to be somewhat lacking in vitality and character. I ascribed this, however, to the fact that I was a stranger to her (remembering that she had been a mere girl when I saw her last in India) and her tongue was therefore somewhat constrained by my presence.

The four of us, that is to say, the two Warburtons, Purcell, and myself, took tea, elegantly presided over by Alice. Colonel Warburton proved to be as genial and hospitable as could be desired, and I could detect no trace of the derangement that Purcell had reported to me. The topics ranged from our time together in India to the life of a general practitioner in London. At my earnest request to Purcell, made as we were travelling down on the train, the name of Sherlock Holmes and my association with him were not mentioned.

As we were finishing our repast, the parlourmaid announced the arrival of Mr Guy Chelmy. I was interested to see the man, given the account I had received of him from Purcell. His appearance as he entered the room was not impressive. Before I started to examine the man himself, I noted the reactions of the others in the room to his arrival – a trick I had observed Holmes use on past occasions.

"You can often learn more about a man, Watson," he

had remarked to me once, "by watching those around him than you can by watching the man himself."

Colonel Warburton, I saw, seemed to find Chelmy's presence somewhat objectionable, and though he disguised his feelings well, it was apparent to me, at least, that there was something of disgust in the way he took Chelmy's hand in greeting. His daughter, on the other hand, seemed relatively at ease, though there was something in the way that she regarded the visitor that made me believe that all was not as it appeared at first sight. Although Purcell had denigrated Chelmy as a rival suitor for Miss Warburton's hand when he had described the man, it was plain he considered him as such. A thinly veiled hostility underlay his every move and word directed towards Chelmy, belying his earlier statements to me about their relations.

As to the man himself, it was difficult to make any definite opinion about him. His dress was, if anything, a shade too immaculate and fashionable to be considered in good taste, though there was no one single item that could be judged to be so. His manners were likewise somewhat too formal and elaborate for comfort, but there was nothing on which one could lay one's finger precisely in order to justify such a judgement.

As I was introduced to him, a flicker of recognition seemed to show in his eyes when my name was mentioned, but he made no comment. I did, however, notice him occasionally glancing in my direction throughout the conversation in what might be taken as being a somewhat suspicious manner.

After some small talk, chiefly about the difficulty of cultivating orchids, a hobby apparently shared by both Chelmy and our host, the Colonel announced that Chelmy would be joining us for dinner, which was to be served in a few hours, and the tea-party broke up. Purcell announced that he would take a turn in the garden, and Alice Warburton proclaimed her intention of joining him. The effect of this announcement on Chelmy was pronounced. For a second or two his face contorted in a look of hideous jealousy, which passed as quickly as it had arrived. Indeed, had I not been watching him closely, I would not have been able to swear that anything had occurred. It was obvious that, whatever Purcell may have believed, he was indeed a suitor for the hand of the lovely Alice.

However, Chelmy was all smiles as he turned to me and proposed a game of billiards.

"I have hardly played the game since my return from India," I excused myself. "I fear that I will prove a very poor opponent."

"No matter," he replied. "I am sure some of your former skill will return once you hold a cue in your hands once again."

As it happens, I had never been a particularly skilful exponent of the game, though I had spent many hours in the Mess hunched over the green baize, but I assented to his importuning.

As we retrieved the cues from the racks in the well-appointed billiard room, Chelmy suggested a wager.

"Shall we say five guineas a hundred?" he suggested.

"I fear you somewhat overestimate the income of a

general practitioner in medicine," I laughed. "If we are to play for money, I would prefer that we play for somewhat lower stakes."

"Ah," he replied, his eyes twinkling. "I had assumed that the chronicler of so many interesting adventures would have received suitable compensation for his labours. My apologies for that mistaken assumption." So saying, he sketched a sort of half-bow, somewhat un-English in its execution. It was obvious, therefore, that he was aware of my association with Holmes.

We agreed on the terms on which we would play, and the game began. As Chelmy had predicted, some of my original skill with the cue returned, but even had I played with the full dexterity of which I had been capable in my younger days, it was clear that I could never have been a match for my opponent, who was a master of the table. Throughout the game, he persisted in making oblique allusions to my friendship with Sherlock Holmes, but I refused to enlarge on the subject. My feelings were that this strange affair of Colonel Warburton's behaviour was in some way connected with this man, and I had no wish to vouchsafe to him more than was necessary in order to maintain a semblance of politeness.

At the end of the third frame, which ended as disastrously for me as had the previous two, I called a halt to the game.

"No matter," he replied, pocketing the modest winnings that I had handed to him. "I trust that the game was not too painful for you," he said, with a smile that had more of cruelty than humour to it.

"Not at all," I replied. I fear my own answering smile was rather forced, not so much at the financial loss I had just incurred, which I could easily afford, but at the insolence of the man, which had expressed itself in many little ways as we had played our game. It is not often that I take a dislike to a man after so short an acquaintance, but there was something about Chelmy that I found distasteful, but whether it was his heavily pomaded hair, or his patent-leather pumps, or indeed, a combination of these and other factors, I was unable to decide. I found it strange, however, that such a man should apparently be an intimate of the Colonel, who was of quite a different calibre.

We parted, I to dress for dinner, and he to the drawing-room where, I have no doubt, he hoped to encounter Alice alone, since we came across Purcell on his way to his room, on the same errand as myself.

I changed quickly, providing myself with sufficient time to write a few lines to Holmes concerning the events of the afternoon, and my impressions of the protagonists in the piece, which I slipped, together with a florin, to the house-maid as we went into dinner, with the request that she post it as soon as was convenient.

Dinner consisted of a delicious mutton curry, of which the three Indian veterans partook with gusto, recalling similar dishes that had been served in Messes in the past as they did so. I noticed that Miss Warburton appeared not to care for the dish, but that Chelmy ate as heartily as the Colonel, Purcell and myself, notwithstanding his lack of an Indian background.

The atmosphere round the table was charged. Chelmy

definitely appeared as the odd man out, not merely on account of the fact that he was the only one never to have lived in the East, but because the other members of the party seemed to be bearing some sort of animosity towards him. On Purcell's part, this could well have been the jealousy I had noticed earlier, and Alice Warburton's mysterious attitude still apparently prevailed. I have already spoken of my own feelings, and Colonel Warburton, though remaining perfectly civil, nonetheless managed to convey a sense of displeasure at sitting at the same table as Chelmy. The man himself behaved as if he were unaware of the others' attitudes towards him, and remained unconcerned, continuing to laugh and tell stories, some of which in my opinion verged on being unsuitable for the ears of young ladies.

Since Miss Warburton was the only lady, and she declared herself to be immune to the effects of cigar smoke, the whole party rose and proceeded to the drawing room, where the male members of the party enjoyed some fine cigars provided by the host while sipping a fine crusted port that the Colonel had decanted in honour of his guests. I noticed that the Colonel limited his intake of this noble liquor to a single glass. Alice Warburton provided us with entertainment in the form of a recital of songs, accompanying herself on the pianoforte. To my mind, the choice of material was somewhat on the sentimental side, but it evidently met with the approval of the rival suitors (for so I felt I must now regard them) as well as that of the fond parent, who beat time with his cigar. I continued to observe him, but could see nothing out of the ordinary that could account for the strange behaviour of which I had been informed.

The music put an effective brake on any conversation, which may have been all to the good, given the potentially stormy atmosphere that had been building up during the meal, and very soon after the last song, Chelmy rose from his seat and with one of his over-courtly bows, announced his intention to quit our company. Wishing him a good night and a safe return to his own house, the Colonel saw him to the door, and then returned to us.

"I must retire to bed, Papa," Miss Warburton said to him. "I am sure that you three Indians have much to talk about. Please do not keep him up too long, Mr Purcell and Dr Watson. I know how you men can be when you start on your memories." She smiled a smile that would have melted the heart of a statue, and Purcell wilted visibly under its force. "Good night to you all."

As she had predicted, the talk soon turned to our Indian adventures, and talk of comrades, some still alive, and some, sadly, now gone before. Purcell had been applying himself to the port, which, truth to tell, was of a fine quality, and it was this, I fear, that led him to his next unfortunate observation.

"But of all the acquaintances that we have made over the years, I venture to suggest that the doctor here has the most interesting friendship of any man in this room," he remarked to the Colonel, who said nothing, but merely raised his eyebrows in response.

I looked at Purcell and silently mouthed a command

to him to cease, but he appeared blind and deaf to all such hints.

"Yes, our old sawbones is the John Watson who writes about the celebrated bloodhound in human form, his good friend Mr Sherlock Holmes."

The effect on the older man was dramatic. He turned to me and glared furiously. "Upon my word, sir! I had no idea that you were some sort of police spy. Were it not for the lateness of the hour, and the comradeship of the Regiment, I would have no hesitation, sir, in turning you out of doors this instant. No hesitation, sir!" he repeated. There was certainly anger in his face, and I imagined also that I detected more than a trace of fear.

I started to stammer some excuse. "Sir, my friend Sherlock Holmes is far from being a police spy. It is true that he has worked with the police on occasion, but he has never taken money from the police for his services, and far from being a spy, he is one of the most honest and law-abiding persons of my acquaintance." I was obliged to stretch the truth a little in my last utterance, as Holmes and I had been compelled to step outside the strict bounds of the law of the land on a number of occasions, but always in the interests of a higher Law.

"Hmph," was the only answer I received, but it was followed by a long silence, during which the Colonel appeared to be lost in thought. Eventually he came out with, "I know you of old, Watson, and know that you are a good man. If you give me your word that Holmes is no spy, of course I will take your word for it."

"I give you my word that Sherlock Holmes is no spy,

but is, on the contrary, one of the greatest and noblest men it has been my privilege of meeting."

"That's good enough for me," replied the old soldier, extending his hand to me in a fraternal gesture. "My apologies for the outburst, but you must admit," he chuckled, "that it is something of a surprise to me to discover such a connection so close at hand. Please forgive any harsh words I may have spoken just now to you."

There was now nothing untoward in his appearance or his manner, and I was reminded of the sudden changes in mood that had been described to me by Purcell. "Think nothing of it, Colonel. Such news is always a surprise, even to those with nothing to hide."

"Indeed so," replied the Colonel, and busied himself with relighting his cigar, which had extinguished itself through being left unattended during the recent exchange.

The incident had nonetheless cast somewhat of a shadow over the previously convivial evening, and soon afterwards, Purcell and I both proposed retiring for the night.

"I will stay up for a while longer," said the Colonel. "At my age, you no longer need the sleep to which you were accustomed when younger."

We bade him good night, and proceeded up the stairs. As I was about to enter my room, Purcell tapped me on the arm and gripped my sleeve fast. "I say, old man," he said to me. The effects of the port on his speech were still obvious. "Dreadfully sorry and all that about mentioning your friend. I had no idea it would take the old man that way."

"No lasting harm done, I believe," I replied. "But it is somewhat strange that it should affect him in that fashion."

"Good night, then," he replied, releasing my arm from his grasp.

I wished him a good night and retired to my room. I determined to keep as accurate a record as possible of the events in order to aid Holmes when he arrived. Certainly the sudden flush of anger, together with the fear that I fancied was present at the mention of Holmes' name gave me pause for considerable thought. It was hard to conceive of any reason why my connection with such a well-known defender of justice should provoke such a reaction, other than in an evil-doer, and it was hard for me to cast the Colonel in such a role.

If it had been Chelmy who had exhibited such a reaction, it would have been more comprehensible to me, given what I had seen of the man, but on the contrary, Chelmy had not seemed to shy away from the subject, but had rather appeared anxious to engage me in conversation about Sherlock Holmes.

I changed into my night attire, and threw my dressing gown, a fine garment adorned with bright Oriental dragons and other decorations, a present from my dear wife, around me as I sat at the small table in my room to write my account of the events of the evening, and my impressions of them. It did not appear to me that Colonel Warburton was deranged, despite his earlier flash of anger, but the more I considered matters, the more it appeared to me that there was something strangely unhealthy in the relationship between Chelmy and the Warburton household.

As I was pondering the reasons for my suspicions which, if I were honest with myself, were based on little more than my personal dislike of the man, I heard a strange shuffling sound in the passageway outside my room. Almost certainly, I felt, this was the strange skipping that Purcell had described to me.

Unlike Purcell, I felt myself up to the task of confronting the Colonel unarmed, and I accordingly opened my bed-room door and stepped out into the passageway. As my friend had described to me, Colonel Warburton, clad in a maroon silk dressing gown, was positively skipping down the passageway, with his back towards me. I moved to the middle of the passage and waited for him to reach the end and turn round.

However, some five yards before the end of the passage, he whirled round abruptly, a wide and somewhat aimless grin covering his face. As he bent his legs, presumably to resume his exercise, I rushed forward and laid a hand on his shoulder.

"Colonel," I said. "Is it not time that you retired to your bed?" I spoke in a calm quiet voice, though I was somewhat horrified by what I had just witnessed. However, at the first touch of my hand on his shoulder, he seemed to relax. The tenseness of his muscles visibly departed, and the expression on his face returned to normality.

"Watson, I thank you," he said to me in a perfectly calm voice. "I believe I was having one of my nightmares. They come on me from time to time, and I have found myself in very strange situations, having been sleepwalking while being visited by these nocturnal visions."

"If I were your doctor," I replied, "I would prescribe a mild sedative to be taken before retiring. I am confident you would not suffer in this way if you were to drink chloral or some such before going to bed. May I, as a friend, suggest that you consult your usual physician on the matter at an early opportunity?"

He smiled at me. "Most thoughtful of you, Doctor. I shall do as you suggest tomorrow morning. A very good night to you and my profound thanks and apologies for having disturbed you in this way."

"And a very good night to you," I replied, returning to my room. I recorded the last events while they were still fresh in my mind, adding them as a postscript to my previous writing. Somehow the Colonel's story of nightmares did not ring altogether true. The look on his face had not been one of a somnambulist, and I had never experienced, or heard described in the literature, such a skipping action performed by a sleepwalker. Nor, despite what had been said to me, could I agree with the diagnosis of mental derangement, tempting as it might be as an explanation of the Colonel's extraordinary conduct. More puzzling still, I could not account for the fact that the Colonel was able to sense my presence while his back was turned to me. I had been wearing soft slippers on a carpet, and I had taken great care to make my movements as silent and unobtrusive as possible. After finishing my report, I extinguished the gas, and composed myself for sleep, but lay awake listening for further sounds. After what was probably about an hour of lying awake I had heard nothing, and eventually entered the land of dreams.

The next morning saw me awake bright and early. The events of the previous evening now seemed like a nocturnal fancy, but I had my written account to convince me of their reality.

Breakfast was a cheery meal. The Colonel and his daughter were both in high spirits, and Purcell seemed to have been infected by their gaiety. There was no sign by the Colonel that last night's events had in any way affected him, until he reached the end of the meal, and threw down his napkin with a satisfied sigh, declaring to Miss Warburton, "I will be going to Dr Henderson this morning, my dear, but will return in time for luncheon."

"Is anything wrong, Papa?" she asked, with a note of tender concern.

"By no means, my dear. It is merely that I have had a little trouble sleeping recently, and it occurs to me that chloral drops might be of benefit to me." He turned to me and winked deliberately, but in such a way that I was the only one to observe the gesture.

"Very good, Papa. I shall go to the kitchen now, and give Cook her orders for luncheon?"

"Yes, yes, my dear. Please do that."

"Excuse me, gentlemen." And with a charming smile bestowed on all of us, Alice Warburton left the room.

"Doctor," the Colonel addressed me. "It is not my place to tell you what to do with your time while you are visiting, but I would strongly recommend that you walk to the top of the rise and admire the view of the town from there. It is very fine. I am sure that young Purcell will be happy to set you on the right path."

"I will do more than that," Purcell readily assented. "I am in the mood for some exercise myself, and I will be happy to walk all the way with you."

"Very good," beamed the Colonel. "Please ensure you return in time for luncheon. I am afraid our cook becomes a trifle autocratic at times, and she tends to exercise her dictatorial nature if we are late for our meals."

About thirty minutes later, Purcell and I were walking through the woods at the back of the house. It was a splendid autumn morning, of the kind only experienced in England. I swung my stick with abandon as I strode along the path, glad to be free of the confines of London for a few days.

Purcell burst upon my peaceful musings with, "I heard the old man again last night."

"So did I. I confronted him, and caused him to return to his bed. He explained that he had been suffering from bad dreams, and was sleepwalking. I advised him to seek the advice of his doctor, and told him that I would prescribe chloral in such a case."

"Hence the visit to the doctor this morning?" asked Purcell. I nodded in reply. "And do you believe that he is indeed suffering from these bad dreams?"

"I confess I have my doubts, but this did not appear as derangement or insanity to me."

My companion let out a sigh of relief. "That is good news," he exclaimed. "But there is still the matter of the egg that I described to you, and also of the parade-ground antics."

"I had not forgotten those, and of course, they would

hardly be connected with the dreams. As matters stand, I am unable to form any opinion on those incidents."

We walked on a little further, and Purcell asked me abruptly, "I wonder when your friend Holmes is going to arrive? I rather fear for his reception when he makes himself known."

"He can be a master of tact, never fear."

The view from the top of the rise, when we reached it, was indeed magnificent. Surrey does not contain the most dramatic landscapes of our isles, but it has its own charms. We admired the vista in silence for a few minutes, and then by common accord turned to retrace our steps.

We entered the grounds of Colonel Warburton's house through the back entrance. As we were closing the gate, Purcell gave a cry.

"Hey there! Who's that? Stop there, my man!"

I caught a glimpse of a ragged grey coat disappearing behind a herbaceous border. "Stop!" I echoed, brandishing my stick.

We caught up with the tramp without over-much exertion. He proved to be a tall man, but put up no resistance as Purcell and I laid hold of him.

"Beggin' your pardon, sirs, but I was told to be here."

"Told? By whom?" I asked, relaxing my grip on the rogue's collar.

"By the gardener, sir. I'm just an old soldier workin' my passage, as you might put it, doing odd jobs here and there to earn a few coppers."

"And Colonel Warburton's gardener said you could work here?"

"That's right, sir. He told me to be weeding this flower-bed here." And indeed, the flower-bed to which he pointed did seem to have been attended to recently, and there was a gardening-basket with weeds in it.

"Very good, my man," said Purcell sternly. "But you may be certain that I will be checking your story with the gardener. If I find that you have not been telling us the truth, be sure that I will come back and have you put in charge."

"I have no fear of that, sir," replied the other, touching his greasy cap. "You may ask all you want, and you'll find that I'm in the clear."

"What a villainous-looking rogue," I exclaimed to Purcell as we made our way in search of the gardener.

"Indeed he is. I'll wager he hasn't seen a bath this year, and criminality is written all over his face. It's not my place to interfere with another man's servants, but I am strongly tempted to question the judgement displayed here. Ah, here we are."

I addressed the gardener. "My good man," I began, "we recently encountered some sort of tramp in the garden who is currently employed in weeding the flower-bed by the walled garden. He told us that you had hired him. Would you care to confirm his story?"

The countryman smiled at me. "Why, bless you, sir, that's the truth. He came to me this morning and said he was an old soldier willing to do an honest day's work for an honest day's pay, so my back being not as young as it was, and the weeds coming up as they do, I thought it was to both our advantage, if you take my meaning, sir."

"Do you often do this sort of thing?" asked Purcell.

"Many a time," replied the gardener. "The Colonel's a good master and pays me well enough that I can spare a few coppers now and then. I used to serve under him in India, you know, and he's good to us who used to be in the Regiment. And when I see these younger fellows like the one over there who'd also taken the Queen's shilling in his time, and can't get no steady work, I says to myself 'Edward Soxworth, that could have been you, if the Colonel hadn't given you this job'. So yes, I helps those who's willing to help themselves like the one over there. How was he getting on?"

"I'm no expert in these matters," I replied, "but he appeared to be doing an adequate job."

"Well, that's all right then, isn't it, sir? No harm done, no bones broken. And now, sirs, if you'll excuse me, I have a line of beets to be thinning out." He picked up the handles of his wheelbarrow and moved in the direction of the vegetable garden.

"He may be a poor judge of character," I remarked to Purcell, "but his heart is certainly in the right place."

THE REST OF THE DAY PASSED without incident until about four o'clock, when Purcell and I returned to the house, and joined Miss Warburton for tea in the drawing-room. The Colonel had failed to join us in another walk around the district, though we had enjoyed luncheon together, and he had afterwards told us that he proposed to take a post-prandial nap in his study.

"Maybe I should go and fetch him?" I suggested.

"If you would be so kind, Doctor," Miss Warburton replied. "In the meantime, I will pour your tea."

I knocked on the study door, but there was no answer. I gingerly opened the door, but the Colonel was nowhere to be seen. An account-book lay on the desk, together with a whisky decanter, a soda syphon, and two glasses, both of which appeared to have been used. A search of the other downstairs rooms failed to discover any trace of the Colonel. I returned to the drawing-room to inform the others of my fruitless quest.

"Maybe you should see if he is in one of the upstairs rooms, Miss Warburton," I suggested. "And in the meantime, maybe Mr Purcell and I should search the garden. If he is not upstairs, your father has probably fallen asleep in the arbour, and needs to be woken."

Purcell and I left our tea and went outside. As we rounded the yew hedge, we saw the yokel who had been hired by the gardener stooping over the Colonel, who was sitting slumped on the garden-seat in the arbour.

"How the devil did you know he would be here?" Purcell asked me, as we started forward to the scene.

"It was pure supposition on my part," I replied. "Stop where you are!" I called to the vagabond. "Do not move, or I fire."

"Do you carry a pistol?" asked Purcell.

"No," I replied in a low voice, "but it will be better if he believes that I do."

The tramp made no attempt to move away, but stood up, and slowly raised his arms, showing that he was unarmed.

"Do not move," I repeated, "or it will be the worse for you." I moved behind the tramp and jabbed my forefinger into the small of his back. Purcell bent over the supine body of the Colonel.

"There's blood here," he exclaimed, looking at the Colonel's head. "This ruffian has obviously made a murderous assault upon our host and was presumably in the act of looting his pockets when we came upon him. I am going to the house to alert the servants and will return directly."

"Is he dead?" I asked. "I cannot see from here."

"No, but he is obviously the victim of a vicious assault," replied Purcell. So saying, he started back to the house.

My Hippocratic instincts overcame me. "I am going to attend to the injured man," I told my prisoner. "I would strongly advise you not to escape, or to make any movement." I bent over Colonel Warburton's unconscious body.

"You need have no fear that I will attack you, Watson." Sherlock Holmes' voice came from behind me, and I spun round. The vagabond was standing tall, and I now recognised my friend under the grime and the shabby rags. He smiled broadly.

"Holmes! How long have you been here?" Though by this time I should have become accustomed to Holmes' mastery in the art of disguise, it was still a matter of astonishment to me that he could so completely throw off his true character and assume a new one so perfectly as this.

"Since this morning, as I explained to you and your friend earlier when you asked me, not knowing that you were addressing me. I must confess," he chuckled, "the two of you appeared to be adequately menacing in your attitudes towards any ne'er-do-well who crossed your path. I quite feared for my safety until I recalled that your Army revolver was safely lodged with me at Baker Street."

"And what are you doing here?" I asked, now having somewhat recovered from my surprise in seeing my friend in this unfamiliar garb.

"The same as you, Watson. Investigating the causes of Colonel Warburton's supposed madness. I merely chose a different path to follow."

"Indeed you did," I replied, smiling. "But what of the Colonel? I find it hard to believe that it was you who attacked him and struck him down in this way."

"Naturally I did nothing of the kind. No-one attacked him. See here." He pointed to a stone by the side of the path with fresh blood staining it. "I call you to witness that this stone is in its original position, and has not been moved recently."

I bent down and examined the stone and the surrounding mould. "I agree with you. But in that case, how—?"

"He was walking and fell, striking his head against the stone. It is as simple as that. I had almost completed my honest labours of the day," he smiled, "and was passing when I observed the accident. My first instinct was to render assistance, and I was just helping the Colonel to a more seemly and comfortable position on the seat, when you and your friend appeared on the scene."

"It appeared to me," I said, "that you were also examining the contents of the Colonel's pockets."

Holmes shrugged in reply. "Maybe that was the case," he admitted. "Today has been an interesting day, and I have learned many things. But maybe you had better attend to your patient?"

"I had almost forgotten." I bent to the prostrate figure and listened to the breathing and heartbeat. "He is unconscious, and breathing steadily. I anticipate no danger, though he should be moved inside the house. But what am I to do with you, Holmes?"

"How do you mean?"

"I was left in charge of a dangerous ruffian who has attempted to murder the master of the house. Purcell will arrive to find me in conversation with my colleague and friend. How am I to explain this?"

"That is easy. You simply point out the stone and the facts of the matter as I have laid them out to you. That should be sufficient to convince even him of my innocence. I, naturally, will remain mute, as befits one of my class, and I will assist in bearing the patient to his house. Then, having received my wages for my day's toil from the good Soxworth, I will depart and make my way to the inn where I will revert to being the more familiar Sherlock Holmes of old."

"That seems to be the wisest move," I replied. On Purcell's return, I explained matters in the manner that Holmes had suggested, and Purcell accepted this account of events readily, as indeed any rational man was bound to do. Holmes and Purcell carried the unconscious

Warburton into the house, where Holmes, touching his forelock in the manner of the yokel whose character he had assumed, left us.

Miss Warburton shrieked a little at the sight of her father, whom we had deposited in an armchair, but I sent her out of the room in search of hot water and bandages.

"A bad business," said Purcell. "Do you think he had a queer turn, perhaps not unconnected with those strange fits of behaviour that have been observed in the past?"

"He may simply have slipped or tripped," I pointed out. "I noticed that part of the path is a little uneven, and the ground is a little muddy at that particular point."

"I wish your friend Holmes were with us now," exclaimed Purcell. "From your accounts, he would be able to take one look at the scene and tell us at a glance what had happened."

"He is not a magician," I laughed. "But he certainly has an amazing faculty for deducing the truth from the most mundane and commonplace of details."

Alice Warburton re-entered the room, together with one of the maids, bearing a tray on which was a basin of hot water, and some cloths to be employed as bandages. I attended to the Colonel, and was relieved to see that his wound was not at all serious, though it had bled profusely. "Do you have some iodine in the house?" I asked Miss Warburton. "I was not expecting to be acting in my medical capacity, and I have no supplies to hand."

"He will recover?" she asked me anxiously.

"I have every confidence he will do so. He has suffered a fall, and has lost consciousness as a result, but his wound, though it has bled freely, as is the nature of such injuries, is superficial." As I spoke, my patient stirred slightly and groaned a little. "See, he is not so badly injured after all," I smiled at her.

"I will help you find the iodine," Purcell offered. "I seem to remember seeing it on a high shelf and I am sure I can reach it easily." They left the room together, and I continued to examine my patient. I was, perhaps, not quite as sanguine as I had appeared in front of Miss Warburton, being aware that injuries of the type suffered by Colonel Warburton can sometimes result in temporary, or in the worst case, permanent impairment of the patient's mental faculties, but in this case I was reasonably certain that the injury was not so severe as to produce such a result.

In a few minutes, the iodine was brought in by Miss Warburton, and the wound now having been thoroughly cleaned, I applied the iodine and bandaged the Colonel's head.

"I would suggest leaving him on this couch," I suggested, "and moving him as little as possible for the next few hours before transporting him to his bed upstairs."

"I will instruct Mary to make up his bed, in that case, to be ready for him," said Alice Warburton.

I looked at her in some surprise. "Surely the bed has been made up already?" I asked. "Mine was, at any rate, when I went to my room after lunch."

"For some reason Papa's bed appeared to be unmade, or at least in disarray, when I went upstairs to search for him. Mary is positive that she made all the beds this morning, though."

"He told us that he was going to take a nap after lunch," Purcell reminded us.

"So he did, but he said he would rest in the study," I pointed out. "Did he make a habit of sleeping upstairs in the daytime?" I asked Miss Warburton.

"No, he never did so," she replied.

I pondered this. After luncheon, the Colonel had obviously enjoyed a somewhat varied afternoon. If the evidence of the glasses on his desk was to be believed, he had also entertained a visitor in his study, as well as sleeping upstairs and walking in the garden. "Were there any visitors to the house this afternoon?" I asked her.

"I did not hear the doorbell," she answered. "And I was in this room almost the whole afternoon." She looked away as she said this, almost as if she had made a confession, but I was unable to fix any reason of this in my mind.

However, even as she spoke, we heard the sound of the doorbell, almost as if to prove to us that if the bell had indeed rung, Alice Warburton would have heard it clearly.

The parlourmaid entered, and announced, "A Mr Sherlock Holmes, madam. Will you be at home to him?" I confess I started to breathe a little easier on learning that my friend's powers of reasoning would be brought to bear on the case.

"Why yes, of course, Mary."

The maid remained in the doorway.

"Well, what are you waiting for?"

"I was wondering, madam, if you wanted me to show him into this room, what with the master laid out there like that?"

"Please show him in here." Her face was set, and a red spot appeared on each cheek as she displayed as much animation as I had hereto seen in her.

"Very good, madam." After about half a minute, Sherlock Holmes was ushered in, clad in his usual London attire. At times like this, Holmes displayed the most exquisite manners, and observing him, one would have thought him to be one of the wealthy idlers-about-town that have so recently been prevalent in the fashionable districts of the metropolis. He introduced himself to Alice Warburton as if she were a princess, taking her hand and kissing it in a fashion that I had never seen him display before.

"But what is here?" he asked, pointing to the prostrate figure of Colonel Warburton.

I noticed Purcell eyeing Holmes curiously and shrugging his shoulders in a sort of puzzlement. "I am sure I have seen the fellow somewhere before," he whispered to me out of the side of his mouth, "but I'll be dashed if I can think where it is that I have met him."

I turned away to hide my amusement, and went over to Holmes. "The patient you see there is Colonel Warburton, who seems to have suffered a slight accident in the garden. I have just finished attending to his injury, which thankfully appears to be less serious than we had at first feared."

"Can he be safely left in the care of his daughter and your friend, do you think?" Holmes asked me. "I would value a few minutes of your time."

"Certainly." I provided Purcell and Alice Warburton with instructions to call me should they observe certain symptoms, and followed Holmes through the French windows into the garden.

"FIRST, I MUST THANK YOU for the excellent report you prepared last night and arranged to have posted to me. It reached me at Baker Street early this morning, and provided me with my ideas of what to expect." Praise of this kind from Holmes was rare, and as such, always welcome to my ears. "If you will tell me what has happened since then, I can likewise inform you of what I have observed."

I informed Holmes of the previous evening's events, as well as those of the day, as observed by myself. He lounged back on the garden-seat, his unlit pipe in his mouth, occasionally interjecting some question.

"You have done good work, Watson," he remarked at the conclusion of my recital. "Your observations certainly provide me with some more definite information on which I may base my deductions. Now I will tell you of my day. I came down from London on an early train, dressed as you see me now, and immediately reserved a room at the local hostelry, where I changed into the character in which you beheld me earlier. Since Colonel Warburton is an ex-military man, I conjectured that he would employ former soldiers as servants, and I accordingly presented myself in the character of one of these when I applied to the gardener for a few coppers in exchange for my services as a labourer. Nor was I disappointed.

"I observed your return from your morning constitutional, as you may doubt recall – no, my dear fellow, there is no need for an apology, as you were only doing what you considered to be your duty as a guest – and I arranged things so that I had a clear view of the Colonel and his guests during luncheon, during which, as you informed me just now, no untoward incidents occurred.

"After luncheon, I managed to find work in a position from which I could observe the study into which the Colonel had retired, though my view was less than perfect, owing to the reflection of the sun on the window. I was, however, able to observe the reception of his visitor—"

I broke into Holmes' account at this point. "What visitor was this? Miss Warburton informed us that she had not heard the doorbell all afternoon."

"I am sure she did not," he replied. "I would not dream for an instant of doubting her word. The Colonel's visitor entered by the same back gate that you used this morning, and was let into the house by the Colonel through the French windows. The two men sat talking and drinking – I observed a soda syphon and a decanter – you mentioned whisky, did you not, when you gave your account of the search for the Colonel – and appeared to be examining something together that lay on the desk. This was presumably the account book that you discovered there.

After about ten minutes the visitor left—"

"Holmes," I interrupted. "You keep referring to this man without even having bothered to provide me with any description."

"Forgive me, Watson, it had quite slipped my mind

to provide you with his identity. The visitor, judging by the description with which you yourself have furnished me, can be none other than your opponent at billiards, Mr Guy Chelmy. As I was saying, he let himself out of the house in the same way that he entered, and entered the drawing-room, again from the garden."

"But Miss Warburton was in there. Surely she would have noticed his entrance?"

"Has she denied his presence? Think, Watson."

"True, she only admitted to not having heard the doorbell. That is deucedly subtle, Holmes."

"To my mind, the whole affair is deucedly subtle. Chelmy appeared to remain in the drawing-room for about ten minutes. I fancied I heard raised voices, but was in no position to move closer without being observed. After he left the drawing-room via the French windows, Chelmy departed the garden by the route by which he had come. While he was in the drawing-room, I had been observing the Colonel seated at the desk, unmoving, with his head in his hands. At this point, I was unsure of his state of health, and I was on the verge of summoning assistance, when he roused himself, and stood up, and left the room, with a somewhat unsteady gait. Tell me, Watson, did he indulge at luncheon?"

"Not at all. Water was the only drink served at the meal, and I will swear he was not in liquor at that time. Indeed, he has become markedly more abstemious since I knew him in India."

"Indeed? Since I saw the Colonel take only the one glass of whisky and soda, we must search elsewhere for the cause of his unsteadiness. After he had left the room, I saw him appear at that window there," pointing, "and shortly afterwards at that one there," pointing to the next window. We will examine the lie of the land up there in a little while, but for now, can you recall the location of those windows?"

"Yes indeed. The first is of the corridor connecting all the bedrooms on this side of the house, and the other is either Colonel Warburton's bed-room or dressing-room – at least the room forms part of his private apartments."

"He passed out of view for about twenty minutes, and I returned to my work among the lupins, while still keeping a watch on the house as best I could. He appeared at the two upstairs windows again, and passed out of sight until he re-appeared in the study. He bent over the desk, and looked at the account-book (or so I suppose) again. Having done that, he passed a hand over his face, and stepped out into the garden with a look of what appeared to be extreme anguish or sorrow. I followed him as unobtrusively as possible, when I observed him stumble and fall. I rushed to his aid, and was then discovered by you and your friend as I was attempting to dispose him in a more comfortable and decorous attitude."

"You also appeared to be searching his pockets when we came across you. What were you hoping to find?"

In response, Holmes pulled a small blue glass bottle from his pocket, holding it with his handkerchief.

"Poison?" I asked, with a thrill of horror.

"Nothing so dramatic," Holmes smiled at me in return. "I had observed this on the desk after the Colonel had made his way upstairs, and it was not there when he came into the garden. The conclusion, therefore, was that he had picked it up on his return to the study, and it was therefore on his person. I felt it might provide a clue."

"And does it?" Holmes unstoppered the bottle and held it out to me to examine. I sniffed judiciously. "Chloral," I confirmed.

"Exactly," replied my friend. "Just as he told you. See here." He once again held out the bottle for my inspection, and I perceived a label, from which I read the name of Colonel Warburton over the name of a Guildford chemist's, with directions for its use.

"So you feel that the Colonel dosed himself with chloral, and this unaccustomed drug produced a feeling of fatigue, causing him to rest upstairs on his bed, thereby causing the disarray that Miss Warburton discovered. Following this, he felt the need for fresh air, and made his way downstairs, and came out into the garden?" I asked.

"Excellent, Watson. I suspect you have made only one error in your analysis."

"That being?"

"That Colonel Warburton did not dose himself with chloral."

"I am puzzled," I admitted.

"And so am I," he replied. "But not about that aspect of the affair. Come, I wish you to show me the spot where you observed the Colonel's eccentric behaviour for yourself last night. Let us enter by the study. That will also provide us with an opportunity to examine the room before some over-officious servant arrives to clear away the débris, and will also allow the young couple to continue their conversation undisturbed."

"I had not thought you such a proponent of romance, Holmes."

He said nothing, but smiled enigmatically in reply, leading the way through the French windows to the study, where his first action was to bend over the two whisky glasses on the table. "Ha!" he exclaimed. "As I suspected. See – or rather, smell for yourself, Doctor. Have the goodness to avoid touching the glasses."

I bent over. "Yes," I confirmed. "One of these contained chloral, without a doubt."

"And I am certain that the one containing the drug was Colonel Warburton's. Let us confirm this. Be so kind as to assist me in this." He pulled from his pocket a small insufflator containing a fine powder, with which he proceeded to coat the whisky decanter. "Only the Colonel touched this while I was observing the two men, I will swear to the fact. Take it up by the neck using this cloth and hold it to the light, Doctor, while I examine it closely," he commanded. He whipped one of his high-powered jeweller's lenses from his pocket, and screwed it into his eye. "Good, good," he murmured to himself. "Now for the glasses." The process was repeated, Holmes making small sounds of satisfaction as he proceeded. "And now," he said, "for the *pièce de résistance*." He removed the chloral bottle from his pocket with the aid of his handkerchief, and let out a sound of satisfaction as he examined its dusted surface. "We have him, Watson, we have him!" His eyes shone with the thrill of the chase.

"Let me see if I can follow your reasoning, Holmes. You know that the Colonel was the only one to handle the decanter, so you are sure of the pattern of his fingerprints. You are sure that only one glass contained chloral, and that was the Colonel's, so the fingerprints on the other are those of Chelmy. You have discovered Chelmy's fingerprints on the chloral bottle, as well as those of the Colonel, no doubt, so you have good reason to believe that Chelmy administered the chloral to Warburton."

"You have followed my reasoning on these points perfectly, Watson. Bravo, indeed."

"And hence when I said earlier that Colonel Warburton had dosed himself with chloral, you corrected me. I take your meaning now."

"Tell me," said Holmes. "Chelmy has never been in India, you say?"

"That is what Purcell told me, and Chelmy never mentioned India at dinner last night when we three old campaigners were swapping yarns of old times."

"And have you observed the Colonel's taste in tobacco?"

"A cigar after dinner last night. That is all."

"So he would be unlikely to smoke one of these?" He held up the end of a cigarette I instantly recognized as a *beedi*, a native Indian form of cigarette.

"Most unlikely," I replied. "And besides, it would be impossible for the Colonel to have smoked this."

"Why?" enquired Holmes, his eyes fairly twinkling.

I perceived that this was some sort of test, which I was determined to pass. "The Colonel has a full moustache, as you no doubt observed, and Chelmy is clean-shaven. No man with a moustache could have smoked this cigarette down to this length."

"Excellent, Watson, truly excellent! And added to the fact that no such cigarettes were to found in the Colonel's pockets, and I see none here in this room, we may conclude that the smoker of this peculiarly Indian form of tobacco is the mysterious Chelmy. He relished the Indian food last night, you said, and he smokes Indian cigarettes. Do you think we can ascribe an Indian background to the man? I think so," answering his own question, "no matter how much he would have us believe otherwise."

"But to what end?"

"Indeed, Watson. To what end? Come, let us upstairs." As we left the room, he picked up the account book

I led the way, and at his request, indicated the position where I had first remarked the Colonel in his unusual nocturnal exercise.

"Facing this way?" he asked, standing on the spot I indicated.

"Just so."

"And you were standing where?" he enquired. I placed myself outside my bed-room door. "What were you wearing?" was his next rather unexpected question.

"My dressing gown," I replied. "Maybe you would like me to wear it now?" I enquired in a spirit of facetiousness. Holmes, however, seemed to take the request seriously.

"If you would be so kind."

Though it seemed to me that I was making a fool of myself, I entered my room and slipped on the gaudy garment. Holmes continued standing with his back to me, however. "Thank you, that answers my question perfectly," he replied without turning. "Now if you will revert to more modest attire, I think the time has come for me to go back to London. I will return here tomorrow. Pray excuse me to our charming hostess, and I would strongly recommend that Chelmy not be admitted to the house before my return."

A FTER HOLMES HAD LEFT THE HOUSE, I made my way to the drawing-room, where Colonel Warburton was beginning to stir a little.

"Where is your friend?" asked Purcell.

I explained the situation, and repeated Holmes' request that Chelmy not be admitted.

"We cannot do that!" exclaimed Miss Warburton. "Why, he—" and broke off suddenly, clapping her hand over her mouth as if to prevent any further words from escaping.

"I'll make sure he does not show his face in here tonight, Alice," Purcell said. "You should remain with your father in any case, and will be in no condition to receive visitors."

Miss Warburton grudgingly agreed to this, and Purcell and I together determined to lift Colonel Warburton into his own bed. He was a large man, but between Purcell's youth and strength, and my experience in dealing with the sick, we managed tolerably well, and were able to transport him to his room without overmuch trouble.

Dinner was a sombre affair. Miss Warburton sat upstairs with her father, dining off a tray, and Purcell and I ate our meal in near silence. After dessert, we heard the doorbell ring followed by the raised voice of Chelmy, and that of the parlour-maid. The blood rose to Purcell's face, and he half-rose in his chair, his fists balled, but as he did so, the noise of the altercation ceased, and we heard the front door close.

"I don't want the brute skulking round the house peering in at us, in any event," exclaimed Purcell, standing up and drawing the curtains. "I'll just do the same in the drawing-room," as he slipped out. The next I heard was his raised voice from the next room, presumably shouting at Chelmy, telling him in the crudest terms to remove himself from the premises.

"All done," he said, returning to the table a few minutes later. "By Jove, I would horsewhip that bounder in a trice were it not for the fact that he is a friend to Alice's father."

I held my peace regarding this last observation, and we moved onto coffee and port. By unspoken mutual consent, we retired early, after first knocking on Colonel Warburton's door, and enquiring after him.

"He is much better," replied Alice. "He is speaking and just seems a little weak. But if you would examine him one more time, Doctor Watson, before you go to bed, I would feel easier in my mind."

I entered the sick-room, and inspected the wound, which was in truth much less serious than we had previously feared. The Colonel, though his voice was faint, appeared to be in perfect possession of his faculties, and I saw no cause for alarm, informing his daughter of the fact.

"Though if there is any change in the night," I added, "you must not hesitate to wake me up and call for assistance."

"I thank you, Doctor, and I also thank you for bringing your friend to this house." She smiled at me. It was an expression that showed the beauty of spirit of which Purcell had spoken, and had up to that time remained hidden from me.

The night passed peacefully enough, and I was delighted to see Colonel Warburton seated at the breakfast table when I made my way downstairs.

"You gave us a nasty turn yesterday, sir," I remarked to him. "I am glad to see you so well this morning."

"Thanks to your skill and Alice's nursing, I feel like a new man," he replied. "Dashed silly of me to trip and stumble like that. I remember it, you know, as if it were part of a dream."

I made some comment, and applied myself to buttered eggs and kidneys. I had just poured myself a second cup of coffee, when the maid announced the arrival of Sherlock Holmes.

"Show the fellow in," said the Colonel. "I shall be delighted to make your friend's acquaintance. Ah, sir," rising to meet Holmes, "I am pleased to see the celebrated friend of Doctor Watson. Have you broken your fast?" waving a hospitable hand at the breakfast table and sideboard.

"I have already eaten, thank you, sir," replied Holmes, "and I would like to congratulate you on your speedy recovery. May I borrow my friend for a while? It is time, I think, that he and I paid a visit to Mr Chelmy."

There was a look of puzzlement, and maybe once again a trace of fear, on the Colonel's face, but he voiced no objection. His daughter, on the other hand, briefly flashed that smile that had lit up her face on the previous evening.

"Come, Watson," commanded Holmes. "Your coffee can wait."

I was somewhat perplexed as we made our way through the suburban lanes to Chelmy's house, the whereabouts of which we had ascertained from Colonel Warburton's parlourmaid. From his demeanour, Holmes seemed to have discovered the answers to all the questions which remained, to me at least, as mysteries.

We walked up the pine-lined driveway to a somewhat ugly red-brick house, set about on all sides by thick evergreens.

"Some men's houses are like their souls," remarked Holmes, but he had no time to elaborate on this observation, as the door was opened by a sour-faced servant.

"Sherlock Holmes and Dr John Watson for Mr Chelmy," Holmes announced firmly in resonant tones. "I rather fancy that he will see us."

"If you will wait one minute, sir," replied the maid, obviously in awe of Holmes' manner. She returned. "The master was just going out, but he can spare a few minutes. I will take you to his study now."

"I fancy he will spare us a little more time than that when he has heard what I have to say," Holmes remarked to me as we were led through the house. "By the way, Chelmy never spoke of his wife, I take it?"

"His wife?" I replied in surprise. "I was under the impression that he was unmarried, and had always been so."

Holmes said nothing, merely raising his eyebrows in response and glancing at a bowl of flowers placed in the hallway.

We were admitted to the study, where Chelmy stood waiting. He extended his hand in greeting, but Holmes kept his hands behind his back, gripping his cane, and pointedly rejecting the courtesy.

"To what," asked Chelmy coldly, obviously more than a little discomfited by Holmes' attitude, "do I owe the pleasure of this visit?"

"I am calling on behalf of Mrs Chelmy," called Holmes. "I find your actions nothing short of despicable with regard to her, as I find your actions in so many regards." Holmes had drawn himself up to his full height, and towered over the smaller man.

A sneer spread over the other's face. "You have no proof!" he exclaimed.

"You think so?" replied Holmes cooly. "Give me ten minutes, and I can convince any twelve good men and true sitting in judgement on you of your nature and your deeds. My proofs are ready formed and fixed in here." He tapped his forehead.

"And what of the precious Colonel Warburton?" asked Chelmy. "Would the exposure not ruin him?"

"I think that is a risk that he would be prepared to take," replied Holmes.

"And his daughter?"

"She will be well rid of you and your evil ways."

"Evil, you say? It is you who is evil, Mr Holmes. Snooping and spying on others, and making wild accusations without proof, and without the force of the law to back you, those accusations are worth nothing!"

I was completely baffled by this exchange, and watching the thrust and parry of the two adversaries left me more than a little confused. "In God's name, Holmes, what do you mean by all this?"

"Behold the husband of Alice Warburton, or, to give her her married name, Alice Chelmy, though I fear, Joshua Hook, that a marriage contracted under a false name is no marriage at all."

For the first time, the little man seemed staggered by Holmes' words. He turned pale and gasped. "How..? When did you find this out?"

"Late last night. It is not so easy to assume a false identity, Hook, even when arriving in England for the first time. There are always the little things. For example..." He pointed to a dagger of Indian design hanging on the wall, with the initials JH embossed on the scabbard.

"That is no proof!" spat the other.

"To be sure it is not," replied Holmes. "I merely point to it as an example of the trail that a careless man will leave behind him. And if you will permit me to observe, Mr Hook, you have been very careless indeed. The account at Armitage's Bank and the other at the City and National, for example."

"How the devil did you discover that?" replied Chelmy, who had now turned almost completely white.

For answer, Holmes pulled out the account-book that I had seen him remove from Colonel Warburton's desk the previous day.

"Aha!" exclaimed the other. "That is your proof? If that book goes, then so does all your proof and so do all your accusations!" He pulled the dagger just mentioned from the wall and withdrew it from its sheath. "Now, Mr Holmes, you will give that book to me." He moved towards Holmes, the dagger pointing at my friend. I started forward, but Holmes waved me back.

"I think not," he said, grasping his cane in both hands and pulling his swordstick apart to reveal a shining slender rapier, the point of which now almost touched the other's throat. "I believe that this blade would penetrate your body and the point would emerge on the other side before your dagger even started to scratch me. Do you wish to make the experiment?" His tone was icy.

Chelmy, or Hook, as I suppose I must now refer to him, dropped the dagger. "What do you want of me?"

"First, I want you to make a clean confession of all your crimes in writing. I then would like you to use the pistol you keep in the drawer there, and to which your hand keeps straying. To use it, I mean, in such a manner as is expected of a gentleman in your position. No, naughty!" he admonished, administering a flick of the rapier to the other's wrist, drawing a little blood and eliciting a howl of fury. "The Doctor and I will wait outside. Come, Watson."

He turned his back and left the room, and after a few seconds, I followed.

"What if he does not do as you suggest?" I asked, when we had closed the door.

"I have no confidence at all that he will carry out any of my requests. He is no gentleman, after all is said and done. I expect him to make a run for it out of the window. Ah, there he goes," as the sound of a window being opened reached us.

"Are we to do nothing?" I asked Holmes.

"We will await developments here," said Holmes with a smile.

I was puzzled, but trusted my friend's judgement in the matter. However, in about five minutes' time, there was a knock on the door, followed by the entry of Inspector Tobias Gregson of Scotland Yard and two constables, with Hook handcuffed between them.

"As you prophesied, Mr. Holmes," said Gregson genially. "The thanks of the Yard go to you, sir. And a very good morning to you, sir," addressing me. "Always glad to see you and Mr Holmes under these circumstances."

"You had deduced, of course, that Chelmy, as he was known, was blackmailing Colonel Warburton?" We were seated in Holmes' rooms in Baker Street, having returned from Guildford.

"I had guessed something of the sort, from the reactions of the Colonel and his daughter. What was the Colonel's crime that put him in the other's power?"

"It was not so much a crime as a deplorable error in judgement. As you saw, Hook, to call him by his proper name, had been in India at the same time as the Colonel, but not during your period of service, and obviously not at the time that your friend Purcell served there, otherwise you would probably have recognised him. You mentioned that the Colonel enjoyed gambling, and you witnessed Hook's skill in billiards for yourself. I have no doubt that he is equally skilful in other recreations, possibly including card-sharping, but in any event, the Colonel found himself in debt to Hook, and unable to repay. Hook proposed a monstrous bargain by which he would accept the hand of the Colonel's daughter in lieu of the money owed, and the Colonel, to his shame, accepted the offer. Hook therefore married Alice Warburton, in his new identity, when he returned to England."

"How did you know this? And why was Alice Warburton living at her father's house when she was married to the other?"

"I suspected it when I first met the lady. I noticed, when I kissed her hand, the imprint of a ring on the fourth finger of her left hand – a ring which had been worn with sufficient frequency and recently enough to leave its mark. I also noticed, as we were being led to meet Hook in his study, a lady's parasol and a pair of lady's walking boots in the hallway. Clear indication that a lady had indeed been present in the house, leaving some attire behind. When I then noticed some flowers in a vase, arranged in a fashion that could only have been achieved by one of the fairer sex, and which was placed on a lace mat – hardly the taste of a man like Hook, you will agree – it bespoke a more or less permanent female presence in the house."

"So Alice Warburton lived as a married woman in that house, except when visitors came to call, when she returned to her father?"

"I fear so. The Colonel would hardly wish to acknowledge a man such as Hook as a son-in-law, and he would have had to provide some explanation to friends as to why a girl like his daughter had married the wretch. I also feel that although Hook had the Colonel in his power by reason of the shameful marriage, the Colonel likewise had some hold over Hook – the fact of his false name, perhaps, and that allowed his daughter to escape Hook's clutches at regular intervals."

"His servants must have been aware of the anomaly – indeed, I feel they were, as they addressed her as 'madam', when I would have expected them to address her as 'miss'," I added. "At any event, she is well rid of him."

"Well rid indeed. Maybe you failed to note the bruises on her arm that I observed as her sleeve rode up when I raised her hand to kiss it. I have no doubt that they were Hook's doing."

"But," I objected, "surely the Colonel must have known that the marriage under a false name was no marriage at all?"

Holmes shrugged. "Maybe so, but that would make the arrangement with Hook even more shameful, and provide even more of an inducement for Warburton to keep the matter hidden."

"I agree. And what of the account-book?"

"The late Mrs Warburton came of a wealthy family, and the family estate had passed to her as the only heir of her parents. When she died, the money passed to the Colonel, who was thereby able to move to England and live in comfort. Hook, at that time unmarried, pursued the Colonel back here, and forced him to keep the bargain that had been made in India – that of marrying Miss Warburton – under a false name. After that, he continued to extort money from the Colonel at regular intervals. The sordid details are all listed in the account-book."

"And the chloral? Why did Hook administer that?"

"I fear that was a clumsy attempt to encompass the Colonel's death and make it appear an accident. My guess – remember, I did not see everything clearly – is that the Colonel had the bottle on the desk in front of him while they talked and Hook, while the Colonel's attention was distracted, added a generous dose to the whisky and soda. Remember, the Colonel was not accustomed to the drug, and its effects, especially when taken with whisky, could easily have caused an accident more serious than the one that actually transpired. There are several reasons why the Colonel's death would have been desirable to Hook. First, the whole of his wife's estate would then have devolved upon his daughter, and hence upon Hook. And also, given that the Colonel had some sort of hold over Hook, any possible menace would have been removed. And lastly, Alice Warburton would then have been his, and his alone."

"But what of the Colonel's madness, if we may term it so? The midnight skipping, the egg through the window, and the farcical parade-ground incident?"

Holmes laughed. "I had dismissed those almost as soon as you described them. What was the common feature of all of them?"

"I cannot say."

"But I can tell you. They all occurred when Warburton and Purcell were alone together, or in the last case, when you and Warburton were together, and there were no other witnesses. Not only that, there were was very little possibility of any other person witnessing these actions."

"I see what you mean. But they were so varied in their form."

"And that is another point that occurred to me. The skipping is a form of mania, the egg incident argues a form of persecution, and the parade-ground a form of delusion. Tell me, is it likely that a patient would suffer from all three forms of insanity?"

"I agree with you that it is unlikely."

"I would go further. I would say that it is impossible. When I further add that no damage was caused to persons or property – the Colonel actually opened the window to dispose of his egg, and carefully closed it afterwards, according to your friend's account – these do not sound like the actions of a lunatic."

"But to what end?"

"Surely it is obvious."

"Not to me."

"Colonel Warburton was well aware of the affectionate

relations between his daughter and Purcell. I have no doubt that in the normal course of events, your friend would have been regarded as an eligible suitor. But since the daughter had supposedly been married secretly, it was obviously impossible for her to have any such claimant for her hand. How to dispose of Purcell without exposing the secret? The Colonel's method was to feign lunacy, in the hope that this would sufficiently dissuade Purcell from any thoughts of an alliance with the family."

"As it very nearly did, and but for your intervention, might well have done."

"I am glad to have been able to play Cupid in this instance," smiled Holmes. "I have no doubt, that once Hook has been brought to trial and his full villainy exposed, Alice Warburton and Philip Purcell may be legally joined together in holy matrimony with her father's blessing."

"I believe that to be a very probable event," I replied. "However, given her previous history, and her past attachment to Hook, Purcell was hesitant to pursue his suit with Alice Warburton further. Additionally, the young lady herself believed that marriage to him was out of the question as a result of her past. Although the couple were obviously very much attached to each other, the problem was to reconcile the unseemly past to a happy shared future."

"A task more in your line than mine, I would imagine," suggested Holmes as he refilled his pipe. "How did you accomplish it?"

"Once I had caused Purcell to understand that Miss Warburton had had no choice in the matter, having been a minor when the marriage was contracted, he began to look on a future alliance in a more favourable light. I also pointed out that the matter had not been noised abroad, and that the so-called marriage to Hook was not only invalid, but was not a matter of public knowledge. This further persuaded him in the direction of matrimony. I advised him to look on the whole sordid affair as if she had contracted an imprudent marriage to a man who had died shortly after the wedding. Although his regard for the Colonel has somewhat diminished, he accepted the force of my arguments. As for the bride, I used similar reasoning to persuade her that she was worthy of Purcell's hand."

"And this was sufficient to bring them together?"

I smiled broadly. "My dear fellow, you are without doubt the greatest analytical detective that has ever lived, and when it comes to matters of pure reason and deduction, you have no peer. In affairs of the heart, though, you must confess that I am your superior."

"I freely admit it," he chuckled. "Pray tell of the presumably vital part of the story that you consider eludes this cold reasoning machine seated before you."

"The vital part, Holmes, is that these two young people loved each other sincerely and passionately. The point that tipped the scale for both parties was my suggestion that they would never find true happiness with any other partner. On considering this, the two flew – I speak metaphorically, of course – into each other's arms. Both of them expressed their sincere gratitude through me to you for your role in exposing Hook and bringing them together."

"It was a relatively trivial affair, once I had visited the house and seen for myself how things lay." He picked up his newspaper, and commenced scanning the agony column, while I continued to ponder the events of the past few days.

"One last question, Holmes. When I encountered the Colonel skipping down the passage, he turned to meet me, even though his back was turned. How did he accomplish this?"

Holmes threw back his head and laughed. "That, my dear Watson, is something I am surprised you have not deduced for yourself. Think back to the night in question. Imagine yourself looking down the corridor at Colonel Warburton's retreating back. What is in front of him and you?"

"A window, without the curtains drawn."

"Quite so. And what were you wearing?"

"That bright green Chinese dressing gown I showed you the other day." I smote my brow. "Of course! He saw my reflection as in a mirror. I should have realised that."

Holmes smiled tolerantly. "Maybe you should have done so, Watson, but do not belabour yourself for it. I have to confess that without your active cooperation and assistance, this case would have taken longer to solve than it did. Indeed, without the assistance you provided, it is questionable whether it would have been solved at all."

At this, which ranked among the highest praise that Holmes ever bestowed on me, I felt a glow of not unjustifiable pride, which was renewed some months later when I attended the wedding of Philip Purcell and Alice Warburton in the capacity of best man.

Sherlock Holmes & The Mystery of The Paradol Chamber

Editor's Notes

The events described in this case, alluded to elsewhere but not described by Watson, show an interesting interplay between Holmes and the official police in the shape of Inspector Tobias Gregson, one of the more capable Scotland Yard detectives, according to Holmes.

Even given that Holmes' appraisal of members of the official force was largely dependent upon their willingness to listen to him and take his advice, it does appear in this instance that Holmes was correct in his judgement. Gregson shows himself at his best here, but it is no surprise, given the final result of the case, that Watson suppressed the release of the details of the case (the manuscript in the deed box was contained in a sealed envelope) – they could well have led to an official reprimand or worse for Gregson. Holmes also shows a sympathy and human side to his nature that is not commonly encountered in Watson's accounts, as well as an irritability that so often seemed to infuriate Watson. Here, then, is the Mystery of the Paradol Chamber.

MY GOOD FRIEND, the consulting detective Sherlock Holmes, was blessed with an almost perfect memory, which allowed him to collect facts and arrange them in such a way that he was able to recall them almost instantly when the occasion demanded. This had been brought home to me in a number of instances, but I had never fully appreciated the force of his mind until the day that brought the business that I have termed the "Mystery of the Paradol Chamber" to his attention.

It was one of those English June days which are more like a return to the days of March than the season indicated by the calendar. The temperature was unpleasantly cool, the sky was grey, and the rain, blown horizontally by the wind, lashed the almost deserted streets of London.

I was at that time lodging with Holmes, my wife having taken herself to the waters of Baden-Baden. I had been prevented from accompanying her on account of my old war wound, which had flared up painfully a little before the time of her departure, and it was a convenience, as well as a pleasure, for me to accept the hospitality of the great detective, and resume our bachelor existence at 221B Baker Street.

I was idling away the time by examining Holmes' library and beginning a re-ordering of his books, which appeared to be in no particular order, making it impossible to locate any desired volume. He, for his part, was standing by the window, watching the rain, and whatever passers-by were braving the weather.

He turned in my general direction. "Please do not disturb the order of the books, Watson. I may need to consult them at some time in the future, and I have no wish to dissipate my energies in searching in unfamiliar places for my old friends."

"But Holmes," I remonstrated. "These books are in no rational order. They are arranged neither by subject, nor by author, nor in any fashion that I can discern. There is no possible way that you can know where they are."

"On the contrary," he retorted sharply, "I have a full and complete knowledge of the contents and arrangement of the books on my shelves, as I will now demonstrate to you, needless though it is for me to do so." So saying, he turned his back to me. "Pray supply me with a shelf and the position of a title on it."

"Such as the third shelf down in the left-hand bookcase, and the fifth title from the left?" I suggested.

"Exactly like that," he replied without turning. "Hartupp on Probate. It is a red cloth-bound quarto edition."

"Very good," I replied, not a little astounded. "The fifth shelf down on the right-hand case, and the second volume from the right?"

"The 1872 edition of Debrett's, in the usual binding."

"It is indeed. And the bottom shelf of the same case, tenth from the left?"

"Bullock and Turner on Deep-sea Pacific Fishes. Cloth-bound in tan buckram," he replied promptly. Now," turning to face me, "please have the goodness to restore order from the chaos into which you have placed those first volumes you have removed from the shelves. Aha!" he exclaimed, breaking off from his criticism of my attempts to act as a librarian. "This is a strange sort of client, to be sure." The bell downstairs rang as he spoke, and I could hear the landlady, Mrs Hudson, admitting a visitor. Shortly afterwards, the door opened to admit a Romish priest, a class of individual who had not, to my knowledge, previously graced the portals of Holmes' establishment.

"Well, Father Donahue," said Holmes genially, "it is a foul day, to be sure. It must have been a cold walk from Euston. Will you take tea, or something a little stronger?"

The priest gave a start. "How in the world would you

be knowing my name, Mr Holmes? And how did you know that I had walked from Euston station and I had not taken a cab or an omnibus, or even the Underground railway?" These words were delivered with more than a touch of an Irish brogue.

Holmes smiled. "As to the last, I see the stub of a return ticket from Watford protruding from your waistcoat pocket. That gives me Euston station. I know that you did not arrive by cab, because I observed you from this window here. The state of your coat and your umbrella – pray give them and your hat to Watson here – leads me to believe that your method of transport was the old standby of Shanks's mare."

"Very good, Mr Holmes," replied the priest, divesting himself of his wet things. "But my name? How do you know that?"

"Even if it were not stitched into your umbrella, Father, I should be a dullard indeed if I could not remember the name of the incumbent of that fine piece of architecture in the Gothic style, Holy Rood Church in Watford."

The little priest stared at Holmes as if at a ghost. "By the living God, Mr Holmes, do you keep a knowledge of the names of all the churches and their priests in the land in that head of yours?"

"No, no," laughed Holmes. "Only of those in the Home Counties." Father Donahue still appeared staggered by Holmes' coup. "But make yourself comfortable, Father, and name your choice. It is a cold day, and I myself will indulge in a small brandy and soda, despite the hour."

"If there is a drop of whisky in the house?" the priest suggested. "With maybe a little soda water, if you please."

"Watson, if you would," requested Holmes. I sensed that since I had been cast in the role of servant, being somewhat out of favour as a result of my attempts to rearrange Holmes' books, but I bit my tongue and said nothing as I prepared the drinks.

"Your very good health, gentlemen," proposed the Irishman as he raised his glass to us. We returned the toast, and the ruddy-faced Catholic priest, clad in the sober black of his calling, sipped his drink.

"You require assistance?" enquired Holmes.

"You once acted for one of my flock, Mr Charles Underhill, in a matter of some delicacy, and he spoke most highly of you on that occasion. I remembered this when this business on which I am visiting you became apparent."

"Ah yes, the affair of the missing emerald brooch. The milkman was the guilty party there, I recall. I must warn you, though, that I am more a practitioner of criminal than of canon law, and my theological skills are sadly limited."

The priest smiled. "Mr Holmes, I have a dark suspicion that your skills in criminal law are what are required here. The theology you may leave to me. Have you ever heard of the Paradol Chamber?"

Holmes shook his head. "I am aware, of course, of the unfortunate French writer Lucien-Anatole Prévost-Paradol. But that is the extent of my knowledge regarding the name. Please tell your story."

"I am, as you are aware, though the Lord God Himself knows how you manage to keep such things in your head, Patrick Donahue, the priest of Holy Rood Church in Watford. It is a very quiet parish, and my flock is a small, but devout one. Among my parishioners is an elderly gentleman, a Mr Francis Faulkes. He is descended from one of the great Catholic families of England, and his line has never veered from the True Faith. He is given out to be very wealthy, and his gifts to the church over the years have indeed been extremely generous. In the past he has given me to understand that on his death, his considerable estate will be left to Holy Rood Church for the construction of a Lady Chapel. He has never married, and to the best of my knowledge, he has no close relatives who would make a claim on the estate."

"This would be a considerable sum of money?" asked Holmes. "Father, your glass is empty. Watson," he half-commanded. I re-filled the cleric's glass, and he continued with his story.

"It would, to be sure. I have not made an exact calculation, but thirty thousand pounds in cash, in addition to the proceeds of the sale of his properties, would not seem to be an unreasonable estimate."

"That is indeed a substantial sum," agreed Holmes. "How old is this Mr Faulkes, and what is his current state of health?"

"He is about seventy years old – in fact, seventy-one according to the parish register – and he is in excellent health. I am no physician, but to my eyes, he has many more years to enjoy before he quits this world."

"And this Mr Faulkes is the root of your problem?" enquired Holmes.

"I would not go so far as to say that," replied the priest. "His money is almost certainly at the heart of the matter, though. *Radix malorum est cupiditas.*"

"'The love of money is the root of evil'," Holmes translated. "Yes, I think that is one point where you and I would agree, Father," he smiled. "There are others, I take it, who also have an interest in this affair?"

"This is so. And this is where the group I mentioned earlier, the Paradol Chamber, enters the tale. Just over one month ago, Mr Faulkes appeared at Confession. As you know, my lips are sealed as to what he confessed as his sins. They were venial ones, to be sure, but I gave him a light penance for his misdemeanours, and pronounced Absolution. Following this, he and I were left alone together in the church, and he asked if he could talk to me on another matter. A priest's ear is open to all in distress, and he informed me of some printed matter in the form of leaflets that he had received from a group calling itself the Paradol Chamber. These leaflets appeared to contain threats to his life."

"Were these direct threats?" replied Holmes, who had been lounging languidly in his chair at the start of this recital, but now appeared to be galvanised into some sort of interest, and sat forward, all attention. "Pray proceed, and describe these leaflets, if you would."

"Each consisted of a single sheet of paper, printed neatly and precisely. I have, as you can imagine, very little experience of this kind of affair, but my knowledge of these matters," here the priest appeared a little embarrassed, "gained, I grant, only from popular fiction such as is printed in the weekly magazines, would seem to indicate that such communications are usually hand-written. They appeared to be direct threats, to answer your first question just now."

"How did Mr Faulkes come by these leaflets? Were they delivered by post?" asked Holmes.

"Now, Mr Holmes, you have hit upon one of the wonders of the thing. Mr Faulkes discovered them in his missal when he attended the Sunday Mass."

"So are we to assume that others in the congregation also encountered these leaflets, or is Mr Faulkes the only recipient of this mysterious group's attentions?"

"If they did, none has ever told me of them. Indeed, I have asked several of the more reliable members of my flock, discreetly, you may be sure, whether the name of 'Paradol' meant anything to them. None claimed to have heard the name before."

"Most interesting," replied Holmes. "How many of these have been received so far?"

"Four, one on each of the previous Sundays up to now."

"All the same?"

"They all convey the same message in principle, but the wording differs slightly in each case."

"And does Mr Faulkes always occupy the same place at Mass?"

"Yes, he does."

"So the leaflets would seem to be placed in advance for him and him alone to discover. I see. Who has access to the church before your service?"

The priest smiled. "The whole town. The House of God is always open for private prayer."

"Quite so, quite so," Holmes murmured. "Do you happen to have one of these leaflets with you?" he asked.

The priest smiled. "I had a premonition that you would ask for that," he replied. "I therefore obtained one of these from Mr Faulkes on the pretext that I would examine its content in order to determine its content and meaning more exactly. He was somewhat reluctant to pass it to me at first, but in the end he relented."

"Your foresight is commendable," smiled Holmes, taking the envelope that the cleric held out to him, and extracting a half-sheet of printed foolscap. "Watson, let us have your opinions on this first."

I determined to show my abilities in the field, since Holmes appeared to be desirous of exposing me in front of our visitor as some sort of revenge for my previous actions. As it happened, my service in India had provided me with the opportunity of playing an active role in the production of the regimental gazette, and I was therefore familiar with the materials and techniques used by printers. Taking the paper, I caught hold of one of Holmes' lenses from the desk, and proceeded with my examination. "Excellent quality laid paper," I pronounced. "High quality rag paper with a watermark that I do not recognise, but if I had to make a pronouncement, would guess was French." I applied the loupe to the printing. "Letterpress printing rather than lithography, and quite probably a hand-press – there is an unevenness that would not be apparent with a stereotype or a mechanical press. The typeface itself is unfamiliar to me, but I think it is almost certainly Continental." I passed the paper to Holmes.

"The typeface is Bodoni," said he with a glance. "The paper is, I think, Italian, from what I can make of the watermark. If you will have the goodness, Watson, to pass me the seventh book from the left on the second shelf of the central case," and there was a somewhat malicious twinkle in his eyes, "I can confirm this. As to the rest, I concur fully. Excellent observations, Watson, I must admit."

I passed the volume, which proved to be a directory of European paper manufactories, to Holmes, who flicked through the pages, and sat back, satisfied. "Yes, Italian, from a manufactory near Rome. Antodelli e Fratelli. As to the content," he reapplied himself to an examination, "this is definitely interesting. 'You will have the goodness to return to us what is not yours to hold and retain and what is rightfully ours. If you do not do this thing, it is our advice to you that you make your peace with God, for then you will surely meet Him soon'. Signed, if we may term a printed line of type a signature, 'The Paradol Chamber'." His face took on an expression of seriousness. "The others all contained a similar message, you say?"

"That is so."

"And there have been four so far? What place does this particular example occupy in the series?"

"It is the third, the one before last."

"Has the tone, or the urgency contained in the message, increased, do you feel? Has the level of threatened danger to Mr Faulkes increased, in your opinion? I see no time or final date by which the demands are to be met."

The other knotted his brows in thought. "I apologise for not being able to bring the others, or to have made notes of the exact wording, but I recollect that they were all much the same. Certainly there was no date or time set for the return of the property mentioned in them."

"Has he, or have you, contacted the police in this regard?"

"I have not done so, and I am reasonably certain that he has not, or he would not have come to me, I feel. This could, after all, be no more than a prank of some kind, though it would be a poor sort of joke, and it would hardly reflect well on me or Mr Faulkes if we were to waste the police's time with some sort of hoax."

"True," replied Holmes. "However, the threat contained in these missives would appear to be of serious intent. Although, based on my past experiences, the official police would have been unable to discover the origin of these messages, they would nonetheless have been able to provide some kind of protection against attacks to Mr Faulkes."

"You take this matter seriously, Mr Holmes?"

"Threats of this nature are never to be dismissed lightly, Father. It may be, as you say, a hoax of a particularly repellent kind, or it may have a murderous intent behind it. As for the item or items referred to in the message, you have no idea to what this refers? He has not mentioned anything of this to you?"

The other shrugged. "I cannot say. He is well-known as a collector of antiquities, but I have never even entered his house, so I cannot say for sure on what basis this is said, or what manner of old things he collects."

"If those reports are true and we are to believe this ,"

replied Holmes, "then we may consider that he has acquired some kind of antiquity to which others may claim ownership, but whether this acquisition is legitimate or otherwise, we have no way of knowing." He regarded the piece of paper once more, and frowned at it. "Though there are no mistakes of orthography here, somehow this does not appear to me to be written by an Englishman. I would also note that the way the longer words are broken at the end of lines does not follow English printers' practices, but would seem to argue a Latin touch. We may be relatively certain, Father, that your parishioner is receiving his messages from an Italian – possibly even from Italy or Rome. Has Faulkes travelled abroad a good deal?" asked my friend.

"Why, yes, to be sure he has. He has taken an Italian holiday at least four times in the past ten years since I have been priest at Holy Rood. Possibly even five or six, now I come to recollect matters more clearly. I believe he was once received by the Holy Father himself at the Vatican."

"Those trips abroad would argue in favour of the theory of a purloined antiquity or some such, would it not?" Holmes examined the printed matter once more. "As I said, I have never heard of this 'Paradol Chamber' that claims to be the author of this document, but I would like to look into the matter a little more. Would it cause you or Mr Faulkes any inconvenience if I were to retain this paper for a while?"

"By no means," replied the priest. "I can easily explain to Mr Faulkes that the document is being scrutinised by an expert, and in truth, I would sooner the devilish thing were as far away from me as possible." He sat forward in his chair, obviously much agitated, and made the sign of the cross.

"You believe the origin to be diabolical, then?" Holmes replied, obviously amused. "I smell no brimstone, and I see no marks of the Devil's hoof."

"It is no joking matter to me, Mr Holmes, no matter what you may think. Believe me, I have seen the Devil at work, and I believe these papers to be part of his doing."

Holmes leant forward. His tone was now serious. "Father Donahue, I take your meaning. I too have witnessed evil at work, even if I do not see a personification of evil such as the Devil in those instances. I apologise if I have offended your beliefs. I too believe there is some evil – I will not use your terms here – afoot, and I will gladly aid you in discovering it, and laying it to rest."

"Thank you, Mr Holmes. You put my spirit somewhat at ease with those words. With your permission, gentlemen, I see that the rain has slackened a little, and I will take my leave of you and wish you both a very good day. Having witnessed your knowledge and memory, Mr Holmes, I will not leave my card, as I am now certain that you need no such reminder of how to communicate with me." He smiled. "You will no doubt let me know as soon as you have come to any conclusions."

"Indeed I will," smiled Holmes, rising, and seeing our visitor to the door. "Well, Watson, what do you make of this?" as the door closed behind Father Donahue.

"I know not," I replied. "I can make nothing of it

other than what has already been mentioned and what I observed for myself."

"Your observations on the paper and printing, if you will allow me to say so, were of a particularly high order and display a true understanding of the subject. Where, if I may ask, did you acquire that knowledge?"

I explained my previous experience in the field. "Although I was not responsible for actually setting the type, or for the operation of the presses, I learned enough to be able to direct the printers in their task," I concluded.

"You never fail to amaze me, Watson. Hidden depths, hidden depths. I congratulate you on your observations, and your analysis, as far as it goes, is excellent. It seems to me, though, that the direction of your thoughts may be the wrong track for us to follow. Fascinating as those details may be, I think that the paper and the peculiar Continental printing are dust thrown in our faces to confuse us. Whoever has prepared this has done his work thoroughly, it must be admitted."

"What do you suspect?"

"I have to think about the matter and consider it more deeply. The matter may be more complex than the worthy son of Erin who visited us just now believes." He paused. "Would you be averse to dinner at Alberti's tonight, Watson? Or will Mrs Hudson's simple English fare be sufficient."

"That sounds like an excellent plan to me. As the reverend gentleman remarked, the weather continues to improve, and the walk to Alberti's will do us good and enliven our appetites."

As we took ourselves to the restaurant that evening, Holmes maintained a silence as we strolled through the wet streets. I guessed that he was thinking of the problem that had been presented to us earlier in the evening, but in the restaurant, as we were tackling the soup, he started to discourse on medieval manuscripts, and the methods used by the monks of that era to produce the fantastical decorations that adorned their work. To hear him talk, one would have believed him to be a scholar who had devoted his life to the study of the subject, rather than an amateur who had only recently taken an interest in the matter. From that, he passed to a discourse on the art of violin manufacture in the eighteenth century, and a comparison of the glues used by the various craftsmen of Cremona.

"Holmes," I expostulated at last. "You are, without a doubt, at the same time both the most fascinating and the most infuriating man of my acquaintance. This afternoon we were presented with a problem, on whose solution apparently hangs the life of a man, and you prattle of fiddles."

"It is not wholly without relevance," he admonished me mildly. "A detailed knowledge of antiquarian matters would seem to have some application to this case. In any event, since these messages have been appearing over the past four weeks, I feel there is no need for me to act with any urgency in this matter."

Holmes was not often mistaken in his reasoning, and he usually felt it as a grievous blow when his foretelling of events failed to come to pass. So it was in this case of his predictions regarding the mysterious messages sent to our visitor's parishioner.

The next morning saw the arrival of a telegram, followed shortly after this by the delivery of the morning newspapers.

Holmes ripped open the telegram eagerly, and I observed his face turn pale with rage as he read it. "Damnable fool that I am, Watson! Arrogant, conceited fool, and worse than that!" He flung the telegram down on the breakfast table and rose to his feet. "If I ever do such a thing again, have the goodness to stand behind me and whisper 'Holy Rood Church' in my ear. The old Roman emperors celebrating their triumphs had more wisdom and self-knowledge than do I!" So saying, he stormed out of the room to his bed-room, slamming the door behind him with a bang that rattled the very dishes on the table.

I picked up the telegram and read the ominous words, "Faulkes murdered last night mysterious circumstances. Request you come to Watford soonest. Patrick Donahue."

I understood the reason for Holmes' chagrin – only the previous evening, he had lightly dismissed the idea of any further developments, and now, a matter of hours after that confident assertion, he had been proved wrong, in the most tragic way. I knew from experience that there was little in my power to bring him to a better frame of mind. Only action was capable of restoring his spirits, and that was a course to be chosen by him alone, and which could not be forced upon him by me or by any other.

I therefore scanned the newspapers, looking for reports of the case, discovering that the Morning Post gave the fullest account.

"Read it to me, Watson," came Holmes' voice through the bed-room door. It took no great skill on my part to deduce that he had perceived my current actions, aided by his acute hearing, which had picked up the sound of the rustling newspapers . I refrained from further comment and commenced reading.

"This is from the *Morning Post*," I began, by way of introduction. " 'We regret to inform our readers of the tragic death late last night of Mr Francis Faulkes of Watford, the well-known collector and connoisseur. Mr Faulkes was seemingly struck down by an unknown hand in his Church Lane house. Mr Faulkes had apparently locked himself in the vault beneath his house where his collection of artistic artifacts and curios was stored for safe-keeping, and was discovered by Albert Simpkins, his servant, following a summons via the house's internal telephonic system. The door to the vault was unlocked and opened from the outside by Simpkins, who discovered his master in a state of collapse, having sustained a severe injury to the head. A doctor was summoned, but was unable to save the unfortunate victim, who succumbed to his injuries within the hour. The police were also summoned, and based on their findings, which have as yet to be revealed to the Press, foul play is believed to be suspected. The celebrated private detective Mr Sherlock Holmes is currently reported to be in Watford, assisting Inspector Tobias Gregson of Scotland Yard, who is leading the case.' There is a little more about Faulkes' acts of recent charity, and a little about his collection. Do you wish me to read these to you?"

"If their information regarding those is of the same standard of accuracy as my supposed whereabouts in Watford, you may forego the pleasure," was the reply from behind the door. "Forgive my vile mood, Watson, if you are able to extend the effort. I am aware that you know me well enough to ascertain its cause, and hope that in this instance *tout comprendre est tout pardonner.*"

"Of course," I replied, and continued to scan the other papers. "There is nothing more of the case in any other of the dailies."

"Gregson's being on the case is a definite positive point. He is far from being the worst member of the Scotland Yard detective force, and he has the almost unique distinction of being willing to learn from others as well as from his own mistakes. If I dare show my face to the Reverend Patrick Donahue in Watford, would you be willing to accompany me?"

"Why do you bother asking me such a question, Holmes?" I asked. "And, if you will excuse me mentioning it, conversations such as this are best held otherwise than through closed doors."

"Very good," remarked Holmes, opening the bedroom door and re-entering the room. I examined him closely, fearing that he might have resorted to his former debilitating habit of injecting himself with cocaine, but was relieved to detect no traces of his having succumbed to the temptation. He noticed my observations and smiled ruefully. "This time, Watson, my vice consisted of no more than mental self-flagellation. I am still cursing myself for an arrogant prideful fool. The least we can do to redress the balance is to take the first train to Watford and lend what assistance we can in the matter. Before we depart, please have the goodness to look up this Mr Faulkes in *Who's Who*."

I retrieved the volume and discovered the entry. "Here we are. Mr Francis Bosforth Faulkes, eldest son of... born... educated Stoneyhurst... served in Grenadier Guards... What information do you wish me to obtain from here, Holmes?"

"Is there any clue as to how he may have acquired his wealth?"

I scanned the page. "He has retained the directorship of several City banks, as well as of a Burmese teak importer, and it would appear that his line, though a cadet branch of the family, has retained possession of a considerable fortune. As the eldest son, he would have stood to inherit most, I would venture."

"Anything out of the ordinary there?"

"I do not know if it is relevant, but he is listed here as being a member of two Catholic orders of chivalry – the Knights of Malta, and the Order of the Holy Sepulchre."

"Neither of those, to the best of my knowledge, has any connection with the name of Paradol, which is still unknown to me."

"Would it be connected with Freemasonry?" I asked.

"That, of course, is a possibility, but it has no place in the Grand Lodge of either England or Scotland – I may say this with certainty, given –" Here Holmes gave me details of the involvement of members of his family with Freemasonry at the very highest of levels, after first swearing me to lifelong secrecy as to the details. Suffice it to say that his source was unimpeachable. "There are, of course, other such movements, unknown to me, where the name may have significance. But come, let us to Watford, and brighten Gregson's day." It was clear that the thought of a problem on which to sharpen his wits, no matter how distressing the circumstances which had led up to it, was proving sufficient to lift Holmes' spirits somewhat.

On our arrival at Watford, we had no difficulty in finding the house in Church Street where the tragic event had taken place. On giving his name to the constable standing guard outside the door, we were admitted to the dining-room of the house, where Inspector Tobias Gregson was seated at the table, examining a pile of papers. A large ledger also graced the table in front of him.

"Mr Holmes," he greeted my friend, with what appeared to be genuine pleasure. "I am glad to see you here. This case is one of the more difficult ones I have seen in some time, and your assistance would be most welcome. And Dr Watson, too. I fear you will not have much to do in the medical line, Doctor, but it is always good to see you."

"It is always a pleasure to work alongside you, Inspector," replied Holmes courteously.

"What do you know of this case?" asked Gregson.

"My sole knowledge has been gained from what I learned from Father Patrick Donahue yesterday, together with the report in today's *Morning Post* which, given that it reported me as being having already arrived in Watford, I take with a very large pinch of salt."

"The Catholic reverend? How did you come to meet him?"

Holmes outlined the previous day's meeting, during which the police inspector made notes.

"That's a strange business, to be sure," he commented at the end of Holmes' recital. "So the old man was suffering from some persecution mania?"

"With some reason," replied Holmes, withdrawing the paper that he had been given by the priest and presenting it to Gregson.

"Well, this is pretty solid," replied Gregson, examining the paper from all angles. "Nothing of imagination about this, is there? Strange paper, and it appears to be an uncommon type of printing to me."

Holmes informed him of what we had deduced of the paper's origins, finishing with, "I think that the origin of this paper may be closer to home, however."

"Who or what is this Paradol Chamber?"

"Alas, I have no information there. Maybe, though, since I have given you the few facts I possess regarding the case, you might be induced to return the favour?"

"That seems like a fair bargain," chuckled Gregson. "I will give you the facts as I have them. Mr Francis Faulkes appears to have been a wealthy man who invested much of his wealth in artistic objects – statues, paintings and the like, most of which are of a religious nature. I cannot pretend to be any kind of expert on these matters, but I believe that some of these are extremely valuable, and some are in excess of five hundred years old. To house his collection, Faulkes converted the cellar of this house into a species of bank vault, with sophisticated locks and alarms.

"It seems that he was accustomed to spend much of his time there, especially in the evenings, examining and cataloguing his collection, and last night was no exception. At eleven o'clock, his usual time for retiring, he had not emerged from the cellar, and Simpkins, his personal servant, communicated with him by the telephonic apparatus installed in the house."

"Ah yes," replied Holmes. "The newspaper mentioned this, and I fear I failed to thoroughly grasp the full meaning."

"It is unique in my experience," replied Gregson, "at least in a private house such as this. Since the door of the vault is so thick, when it is closed it is impossible to hear any sound from outside once inside the vault, and vice versa. Accordingly, Faulkes had caused a telephonic apparatus to be installed, whereby the servants could communicate with him should a visitor chance to call, or should any other matter requiring his attention arise. On occasion, he had been known to fall asleep while in the vault, and the sound of the telephone bell in there, as activated by one of the servants, was then used to rouse him."

"And in this case, it did not?" asked Holmes.

"That is correct. According to Simpkins, the bell should have rung for at least a minute, and since Faulkes was apparently a light sleeper, that would ordinarily have been ample time to rouse him. Simpkins therefore descended to the vault and proceeded to open it."

"One moment," interrupted Holmes. "How is the vault secured?"

"By a combination lock. There is no key. The door can be locked from the inside, and Faulkes commonly did so while he was working on his collection. It was so secured last night, according to Simpkins."

"And Simpkins was in possession of the combination?"

"So it would appear. He freely admits to the knowledge."

"Do any of the other servants possess the combination?"

"Besides Simpkins, the household consists of a cook, a kitchen-maid and a house-maid. There is also a gardener, but he is employed by the hour, and does not live on the premises. The resident servants have been questioned, and all deny any knowledge of the combination."

"Well then, Simpkins entered the vault, and next?"

"He beheld his master lying on the floor, with his head in a pool of blood and a fearful wound that had smashed the right temple like an eggshell. A fallen statue was by the body, with the arm broken off and lying by itself nearby."

"The arm had been used as the weapon, presumably?" asked Holmes.

"Now, Mr Holmes, this is one of the matters in this case that has me puzzled. No, the arm was not the weapon. The statue is that of an angel, constructed of some sort of plaster or other material, and with a solid octagonal stone base – granite or some such. To judge by the blood and hair and so on coating it, one corner of the heavy base had been used to strike the blow. But I am running a little ahead of myself in my recital of events. Faulkes was not dead, but he was unconscious. With considerable promptitude and presence of mind, Simpkins roused the two maids, and dispatched one to the doctor, and one to the Catholic priest who visited you yesterday. He and the cook stayed with Faulkes in the vault, not wishing to risk further injury by moving him, but attempted to make him comfortable. The priest and doctor arrived within the half-hour, but Faulkes was sinking fast. Both did what they could, but the end was near, and the Catholic rite of Last Unction was administered, the dying man being unable to form the responses. In the meantime, one of the girls had been sent to summon the local police, who immediately contacted the Yard. Hence my involvement."

"A pretty puzzle," remarked Holmes grimly. "We have a man in a locked room, with the sole method of entry known to himself and only one other, so far as we can determine at present. The man is struck down by an unknown assailant, who lets himself out of the locked room and locks it behind him again. Tell me, does the lock require the combination in order to unlock it from inside the vault or to re-lock it?"

"That is something we have yet to discover," replied Gregson. "I take your meaning. If the assailant was locked in the vault with Faulkes, could he have let himself out and re-secured the entrance? An excellent point, Mr Holmes." He made a note in his notebook.

"Is the body still in the place where it was found?"

"No, we felt it should be moved, and it is now in the

morgue at the hospital. But," Gregson smiled, as Holmes started to raise a warning finger, "I have profited by my association with you. Before the body was moved, I adopted your excellent suggestion of using chalk to outline its position and attitude, as far as could be ascertained. The doctor had moved the arms and so on to compose the body for death, but I questioned him closely and I am satisfied that I have an accurate representation of the body as it was originally."

"I am glad to see that my teaching has not fallen on stony ground." Holmes smiled. "You will go a long way, Inspector. I foresee a bright future for you if you continue in this way. And the statue?"

"That has remained untouched."

"Excellent. Now to the *dramatis personæ*. What of this Simpkins? How long has he been in his present position?"

"He appears to be utterly reliable in his testimony. He has been with Faulkes for over thirty years now."

"I will want to question him, with your permission," said Holmes. "If I may see your records of your preliminary questions to him, I will avoid duplication, and we may save some valuable time."

"Naturally," said Gregson, pushing a sheaf of papers towards Holmes, which my friend started to peruse. "I thought, however, that you would prefer to see the scene of the murder before anything else."

"Since you have moved the body already," replied Holmes, "there is little advantage to my examining that area immediately. Little will change, after all. On the other hand, the memories of witnesses fade very fast, and it is important to retrieve all those impressions as soon as possible after the event."

"I understand your reasoning," replied Gregson. He asked the constable standing at the door to call Simpkins for questioning.

The man who entered was an elderly man, apparently sixty years or over in age, but still of an upright and sprightly appearance. He was neatly dressed in servant's black, and I noticed that he had already secured a mourning band around his right sleeve.

"This gentleman here is Mr Sherlock Holmes," Gregson said to him by way of introduction. "He is here to ask you a few more questions which may not have occurred to me when I talked to you earlier."

The elderly servant addressed my friend. "I have to confess, sir, that it is an honour for me to be conversing with the celebrated Sherlock Holmes, whose exploits I have admired when I have read about them. However, I sincerely wish that this meeting was under happier circumstances than the ones in which I find myself at present."

Holmes smiled benignly. "Thank you, Simpkins. I will try to make the process of questioning as painless as possible for you. My first question is with regard to the locking of the door of the vault. Is it necessary to use the combination to unlock the door from the inside?"

"Yes, sir, it is."

"And is the combination also needed when the door is to be re-locked, either from the inside or from the outside of the vault?"

"Yes, sir, from both the inside and the outside."

"Inspector Gregson has informed me that your master vouchsafed the combination to you. Has this combination been in your possession for a long time?"

"No sir, he only gave me the combination just over one month ago."

"Thank you. To the best of your knowledge, are you the only member of this household other than your master who had knowledge of the combination?"

"Yes sir, I am certain of it. I had been aware for several years, though, because he had informed me of the fact, that a copy of the combination had been lodged by Mr Faulkes at his bank, and was to be made available to the executors of his will in the event of his untimely death."

"A very laudable precaution," observed Holmes. "Would you care to give us the combination?" The other hesitated. "There is little merit in your keeping it a secret now. As you have just told us, the executor of the will has full access, and it would be a simple matter for the Inspector here to obtain a court order to release it from the bank's custody."

"Very good, sir." Simpkins seemed to be speaking with some reluctance. "The combination is 22-07-18-73."

"Thank you," replied Holmes, as Gregson wrote down these numbers in his notebook. "Inspector Gregson has already informed me of your prompt and meritorious actions following the discovery of your master. Is there anything that you would like to add to those observations? Did your master have any enemies of who you are aware?"

The aged servant shook his head. "No sir, I think that

I have provided as full an account as is possible under the circumstances. Please rest assured, sir, that if I recollect anything further that would seem to further the inquiry I will immediately inform the police."

"Thank you for your cooperation, Simpkins," said Gregson. "Do you have any more questions, Mr Holmes?"

"Indeed I do. Simpkins, can you recollect any visitors who called on your master frequently?"

"Other than the Italian gentleman, you mean, sir?"

Holmes, Gregson, and I exchanged glances. "You never mentioned this Italian gentleman earlier," said Gregson sternly. "Perhaps you should tell us a little more about him."

The other was obviously flustered by this request. "Well, sir, I would hardly describe him as a gentleman, if I were to be completely honest with you. Mr Faulkes was always at home to him, however, and he and Mr Faulkes spent many hours together in the museum."

"Which museum is this?" asked Holmes.

"My apologies, sir," replied Simpkins. "We servants often described the master's collection as 'the museum' in jest. What I meant by my last remark was that Mr Faulkes and his Italian visitor would often spend time with the collection."

"Do you happen to know if this Italian is connected with the antiquities trade?" asked Holmes.

"I have no knowledge regarding that, sir," replied the other.

"When was the last time that this Italian personage came to call?"

"Why, sir, last night."

Gregson started to his feet, his face contorted with anger. "Pardon my language, Mr Simpkins, but blast you, you never provided us with this information when I asked you about the events of yesterday evening earlier. Why did you omit this from your report?"

"I was not completely convinced that it was of immediate relevance, sir," replied the servant.

"You will permit me, Simpkins, to decide what is relevant and what is not relevant in this case," retorted Gregson, subsiding into his seat.

The other looked abashed. "I am sorry, sir," he replied at length.

"If I may?" interjected Holmes. "Simpkins, did you admit this Italian visitor, and did you show him out, and at what times did he arrive and did he depart?"

"He arrived at the house at eight o'clock precisely," replied Simpkins. "I opened the door to him, and showed him into the drawing-room where Mr Faulkes was waiting for him."

"He was expected, then?" Gregson asked.

"Yes, Mr Faulkes had informed me previously that he was expected. He was a reasonably regular visitor to the house. He started visiting the house about four years ago, making his visits approximately once every month, until about a month ago, when he started to visit on an almost weekly basis."

"And what time did he depart last night?" enquired Holmes. "Were you the one who showed him to the door?"

"As far as I could tell, he left the house a little before

nine o'clock. I was not the one who showed him to the door, you should understand."

"You are sure that he left the house?" asked Gregson.

The other replied a little stiffly. "I heard Mr Faulkes and the visitor walking through the hall towards the front door together, engaged in conversation. I heard them bidding each other a good night. I heard the front door open and close, and I heard a single set of footsteps walking through the hallway, and descending the steps to the cellar. I am therefore as positive as I can be that Mr Faulkes himself let his visitor out of the house and returned alone to the vault. I heard the sound of the vault door opening and then closing."

"And you never heard the door open again?"

"No, sir, I did not. The door makes a somewhat distinctive sound when opened, and I am convinced I would have heard it, had it been opened again."

"A most astute set of observations," remarked Holmes. "Did you, by any chance, happen to remark the nature of the conversation that they might have had before bidding each other good night?"

The servant's sallow face took on a faint flush. "I am sorry to say, sir, that I did. Their conversation was in the nature of a disagreement." He paused. "Is it necessary for me to report this to you?"

"It is your duty, man," replied Gregson, sternly.

"I do not know the nature of the disagreement. Believe me, I am not concealing anything in this regard. However, I heard my master saying, 'I must do it tonight. I have no choice.' And the Italian visitor saying, 'It shall not happen tonight, and if I could, I would move heaven and earth to prevent it.'"

"And your master's response to this?" asked Holmes.

"He replied, 'You cannot frighten me further. In any case, my mind is made up.' Following this, he and Mr Paravinci went outside the front door. I assume that they bade each other a good night before Mr Faulkes re-entered the house and closed the front door before going downstairs to the cellar."

"Ha! The mysterious gentleman's name is Paravinci, then?" said Gregson. "Does this personage have any other name, and is there any other information you can give us about him?"

"I am reasonably certain that his Christian name is Antonio. I heard Mr Faulkes address him as such on several occasions in the past. He lives in London, at an address in Whitechapel, which I will recall in a minute, if you will permit me." He paused, obviously in thought. "Yes, number 42, Greatorex Street was the address on the letters to him from Mr Faulkes that I conveyed to the post."

Gregson was scribbling furiously in his notebook. "And his age?"

"I would guess he is in his late twenties. Maybe a little over thirty years of age, but only a little."

"Can you describe him?" Gregson demanded.

"There is no need for that, Inspector," Holmes chided gently. "I am sure we will be speaking to the man himself before too long."

Gregson nodded in agreement, and turned back to Simpkins. "This information should all have been given to us earlier." It was obvious that his anger had only abated slightly. "You are fortunate, Simpkins, that I have not had you arrested for obstruction of justice."

"Come now, Inspector," soothed Holmes. "Mr Simpkins is naturally in a state of some confusion following last night's tragic events." He turned to the servant. "What words would you use to describe the tone of voice that you heard?"

"Although the two were obviously in disagreement, there was no anger on either side. If I were to describe the tone of voice of both parties, I would say it was closer to a form of resignation rather than anger, sir." Simpkins was obviously relieved at not having to face Gregson's wrath further.

"If you had to make a guess as to the meaning of the words you overheard?" Holmes prompted.

"I would not like to hazard any such conjecture," said the other.

"Very good," said Holmes. "I have no further questions at present. Inspector?"

"Nothing at present," echoed Gregson. "Well, Simpkins, I hope that if anything further occurs to you, you will have the kindness to inform me or one of my officers, regardless of whether you consider it relevant to the enquiry or not." His tone was heavily sarcastic, and the unfortunate Simpkins shuffled his feet, and muttered some sort of apology, his eyes downcast. "You may leave us," added Gregson.

"Well, Watson," said Holmes to me after the servant had left the room. "You were silent throughout the whole of that conversation, if I may term it such. What are your impressions?"

"He is hiding something."

"By Jove, without a doubt he is hiding something," agreed Gregson, angrily. "And I am willing to lay money that he and this Italian devil Paravinci were blackmailing poor Faulkes over some petty misdemeanour that took place long ago."

"Blackmail seems to be a likely possibility to me," I concurred. "Holmes, what is your opinion?"

"I agree with you both that Simpkins is concealing something from us. However, I disagree with your conclusion that it is blackmail, though I am at present unable to assign a precise reason for my belief. I am certain that we will never be able to extract the hidden information from Simpkins. He strikes me as being one of the bulldog type who, once in possession of a secret, will never surrender it unless it is dragged out by force. The other servants, what of them?" he asked Gregson.

"You may see their statements here," replied the Scotland Yard detective. "I have no reason to doubt them, but we may summon them for further questioning if you think this would be of value."

"At this point in the enquiry, I will forbear. I think now would be a suitable time to view the scene downstairs. If we could arrange to speak with Father Donahue," he pulled out his watch and consulted it, "in about ninety minutes' time, I would appreciate this. Do you think you could instruct one of your men to arrange this?"

"Certainly we can do that. I fail to see what information

he will be able to provide, though, since he was not present immediately after the attack on Faulkes. I will also send orders for this Italian Paravinci to be brought in for questioning. Does it not seem a coincidence to you that the papers of which you spoke, and a sample of which you showed me earlier are also from Italy?"

"No coincidence at all. But beware of the obvious, Inspector. It can often be deceptive," was Holmes' only comment, as we rose from the table and made our way out of the room towards the cellar.

THE DESCRIPTIONS OF THE CELLAR both as a "vault" and as a "museum" certainly had much to commend them. The entrance to the cellar was guarded by a solid door, some six inches in thickness, and secured by a complex combination lock. Once inside the cellar, I was astounded, as was Holmes, insofar as I could judge by his reaction, by the works of art contained therein.

Three of the walls were lined with glass cases, containing small paintings, works of art, illuminated books from a bygone age, and gold and silver ornaments, most of them with a religious origin. A few weapons, mainly jewelled daggers and the like, also graced the cases. Larger paintings of a primitive medieval style hung above the cases, and though I would not pretend to expertise in the field, they seemed to me to be of Italian origin. The fourth wall facing the door had no cases arranged along its length, but was lined by a row of some dozen statues depicting angels playing musical instruments, each about four feet in height. There was a gap in the middle of the line of statues, and I immediately guessed that this space had been filled by the statue responsible for Faulkes' death.

Holmes stopped in the doorway, and looked around him.

"It is quite a sight, is it not, Mr Holmes?" said Gregson, smiling.

"Indeed it is," he replied. "I am not surprised at the servants' name for this room. This is an impressive door, is it not?" He swung the heavy door closed, and as gently as it closed, there was a distinctive thud as it swung ponderously into its frame. "Let us open it again," he said, tugging at the handle. As the door swung open, there was a loud creaking sound from the hinges. "As the good Simpkins remarked, it is a most distinctive sound, and I am reasonably certain that he would have noticed it had the door been opened again after Faulkes had returned here." He walked slowly about the room, examining the display of curios, his hands clasped behind his back. "Has anything been removed, do you know?"

"I see no obvious gaps in the cases," replied Gregson. "All are locked, and none has been forced. I detect no sign of any object or painting hanging on the wall having being removed."

"You would rule out robbery as a motive, then?" asked Holmes.

"I cannot be completely certain as yet. The ledger upstairs appears to be a meticulous record of all the objects contained in this room. I will naturally have a check made of the contents of the room and compared to the lists in the ledger. I will be surprised, though, if there is any discrepancy."

"I too," remarked Holmes. "However, I commend your attention to detail in making such a check." He broke off suddenly. "How is this room ventilated?" he asked Gregson. "I take it that these gas lamps have been burning continuously since the body was discovered, and therefore since yesterday evening?"

"We have not touched them," confirmed Gregson. "If you will take the trouble to look upwards, you will see a sliding grille in the centre of the ceiling communicating with some sort of vent leading to the outside. It appears that the grille can be opened and closed by this cord here," pointing to a loop of stout sash-cord suspended from the ceiling. "We have not touched this, either. And before you start to go off on one of your theories, Mr Holmes," he smiled, "the vent is a mere nine inches in diameter. I think it is most unlikely that the murderer could have entered and exited the room by that route. There are also two ventilation grilles above the door, leading to the cellar proper. Those are likewise too small for any entry or exit."

"I agree with your conclusions," Holmes replied, apparently not at all offended by Gregson's gentle chaff. "The ventilation has hardly dispersed the smell of ether, though."

"Ether?" exclaimed Gregson. "I confess that I am suffering from a slight cold, and had failed to remark any such odour."

"I can also perceive a slight smell of ether," I confirmed.

"Undoubtedly it is ether, Inspector. No doubt left behind from the doctor's examination of the body."

"No doubt," answered Holmes, absent-mindedly. By this time, he had arrived at the spot in the centre of the room where a chalk outline marked the position of the body as the police had outlined it in the way Gregson had described. A large dark stain marked the floor at the point where the head had lain. "The injury was to the right temple, you say?" he asked. Gregson confirmed this. "So the body was lying face uppermost, if the evidence of the bloodstain is to be believed?" The policeman nodded. "So we may conclude that the blow was struck with the left hand."

"I had remarked that. Simpkins, by the way, is right-handed, as are all the servants in the house."

"Well done, Inspector. Such an early elimination is always of value. Even though you and I still suspect Simpkins of being somewhat less than straightforward, we do not suspect him of the killing, do we? Never fear, we will soon discover whatever it is that he feels he must keep secret from us. There is a considerable amount of blood, is there not? We must assume that a major blood vessel was damaged by the blow. And this," he went on, bending forward, "is the angel of death, if we may term it such."

A shiver went over me as he pronounced this description, and even Gregson, whom I had imagined to be immune to such feelings, appeared to shiver at the words.

"With your permission, Inspector, I would like to remove a sample of the hair and tissue attached to this?" Gregson signified his assent, and Holmes delicately removed a small sample of the gore that was attached to the base of the statue. I drew closer and examined the object more closely. Obviously one of the set of statues by the wall, this particular angel had been in the act of holding a trumpet aloft. The arm holding the trumpet had broken away from the body, and now lay some distance from it among the bloodstains. I examined the arm as closely as I could without touching it, and discovered it to be hollow, and apparently composed of some sort of earthenware, somewhat similar to terracotta, which had been decorated with paint, as could be discerned from the chips of material surrounding it. I returned to the main body, and examined the base of the statue which, as we had been informed, was composed of stone, in the shape of an octagon.

"Let us try the weight of one of these," remarked Holmes, standing up and moving to the wall. He grasped one of the statues around the middle and lifted. "The weight is concentrated in the base, as you might expect," he observed. "In fact, the whole thing is somewhat like a large hammer."

"Somewhat clumsy and ill-shaped, though, as far as any practical purpose is concerned," I pointed out. "Why, the merest blow would shatter the 'handle'."

"Indeed it would, Watson." The idea appeared to give him pause for thought and he strode back to the centre of the room where he stood, gazing up at the ventilator, and down at the chalk outline and the statue and its detached arm. Gregson watched with amused puzzlement.

Holmes returned to the line of statues, and examined

them closely. "This one has been broken and repaired," he noted. "See here, Watson."

I examined the artwork in question, noting that its arm had become detached in much the same way as the one by the body, and had been repaired by a very unskillful hand. "Why, Holmes," I exclaimed, "it seems that the glue used to piece this together is hardly dry."

"Indeed," said Holmes. "Without knowing the exact composition of the adhesive, we cannot tell the exact date at which the repair was carried out, but my impression that it was within the last few days at most."

"I have seen enough here for present. Can you give orders that nothing is to be touched or moved, Inspector?"

"Certainly."

We returned upstairs to the dining-room to find that Simpkins, maybe to make amends for his earlier reticence, had, without being asked, laid out an excellent luncheon of cold meats and salads. We thanked him, and the previous gory scene notwithstanding, fell to with good appetites.

When we were almost finished, and Simpkins had brought in coffee, there was a ring at the front door.

"Ah, the priest," exclaimed Holmes. "I had almost forgotten about him."

Father Donahue was ushered into the room, and persuaded to take coffee with us.

"A tragic business," he intoned, wagging his head.

"And I owe you an apology, Father, for not acting more promptly," replied Holmes contritely. "If I may borrow the words of your Church, with all due sincerity, I pronounce *mea culpa, mea culpa, mea maxima culpa.*"

"There is nothing for which you can blame yourself, I feel," replied the priest. "There was no way that you could have foreseen this."

"Do you have any idea who might have done the deed?" asked Holmes.

"I cannot say," replied the cleric.

"I understand," my friend replied, pensively. "To change the subject, Father, you were with the unfortunate man when he died. Did he utter any words to you before he passed away?"

The other shook his head. "Nothing. He was unconscious when I arrived and was incapable of speech. Thanks be to God, he was at least alive, and I was able to administer Extreme Unction to him. There was no thought of my hearing his confession or his performing Penance or taking the Eucharist. I am certain, though, that he died in a state of grace, and that his soul's stay in Purgatory will be a short one."

Such a discussion of religious matters made me uncomfortable and uneasy, as it would the majority of Englishmen. I noticed that Gregson appeared to share my discomfort, but Holmes appeared to be unaffected by this Romish show of piety.

"And as far as you are aware, the doctor likewise noted no words from Faulkes before he died?" he asked.

"Not that I am aware of. He said nothing to me, if he did. Not that I would expect him to," added the priest, not without a certain humour. "Dr Addison, like so many of his profession, saving your presence, Dr Watson, is a so-called freethinker – in other words, an unbeliever."

"Are you aware," my friend asked suddenly, "of the name Paravinci? Does it mean anything to you?"

"I believe I may have encountered the name," said the priest. "I have worked with Italian immigrants in the East End of London, and the name is not an uncommon one."

"Antonio Paravinci?" pressed Holmes.

Donahue shrugged. "Possibly. Antonio is likewise a common Christian name. I do not have any special recollection of anyone by that name. May I ask why you are enquiring?"

"You may certainly ask, Father, but I am under no obligation to provide you with an answer. Like you, I have my professional secrets." Holmes smiled at the cleric, and the priest, obviously taken with the conceit, smiled in return.

"If you have no more questions," said Donahue, "I must away to my flock. More mundane matters, but ones, I assure you, of equal importance to this affair in the eyes of God." He took his leave and departed.

"A strange fellow, that," remarked Gregson.

"But sharp, for all that," Holmes replied.

"Even though he knows nothing of this matter?"

"He never said that he knows nothing," countered Holmes.

"Did he not? I rather fancied that he did," answered the police detective.

"Consider his exact words to us. Be that as it may," replied Holmes, "I would like to view the body at the mortuary, if I may receive your permission to do so."

"Granted without reservation," said Gregson. "Dr Watson, I take it you will want to be present?"

"Naturally," I replied.

"Good." Gregson scribbled his signature on a piece of paper from his notebook and handed it to Holmes. "Between you and me, Doctor," turning to me, "the police surgeon here strikes me as somewhat of a fool, and I do not altogether trust his conclusions. Your observations would provide me with a more reliable view of the situation."

At that moment, there was another ring at the door, and a constable was admitted.

"Begging your pardon, sir," he addressed Gregson. "We've just had a wire from Scotland Yard in at the station. They have located the Italian party in question, and can be bringing him here within an hour if you wish, or if you prefer, they will hold him in London to wait for your return."

Gregson turned to Holmes.

"I would strongly recommend bringing him here," said Holmes. "If nothing else, he can be positively identified by Simpkins, and we can observe their reactions when confronted with each other if it appears desirable to do so."

"That would seem to be good sense," agreed Gregson. "Ask London to send him up here as soon as possible, in the company of a pair of constables. Also ensure that Sergeant Wilkerson comes here at the same time," he said to the local policeman, who acknowledged the order and left us.

"Who is this Sergeant Wilkerson?" asked Holmes. "The name is unfamiliar to me."

Gregson smiled. "He is a new addition to the strength of Scotland Yard, and something of a rarity in our ranks.

He is a graduate of Cambridge University, and acts as the Force's expert when it comes to questions of an artistic nature, such as forgery or theft of paintings and the like. His rank of Sergeant is a somewhat honorary one. He is no-one's idea of a Metropolitan Police officer, to be sure."

"You intrigue me," replied Holmes. "I look forward to the pleasure of his acquaintance."

"He will be with us within the hour, I hope."

"Then, Watson, let us make haste to the mortuary," suggested Holmes. "We will return in about an hour, or a little more, Inspector, and inform you of our findings."

Upon our arrival at the hospital, Holmes seemed relatively uninterested in the body of Francis Faulkes after the first inspection, concentrating his attention on the contents of the deceased's pockets, which had been sorted and labelled by the mortuary staff.

I occupied myself with examining the body, concentrating my attention on the right temple, where the ghastly wound gaped. It was a little lower down and to the front than I had been led to believe, and the bone around the hole formed by the angle of the statue's base was obviously crushed. I was surprised, given the nature of the wound and the obvious force with which the blow had been delivered, that Faulkes had survived and had not been killed outright. I had borrowed one of Holmes' lenses to examine the details more closely, and as I moved the glass over the dead man's face, I noticed some tufts of what appeared to be cotton-wool adhering to the inside rim of the nostrils.

"Have you cleaned or plugged the facial orifices?" I asked one of the attendants.

"No, sir," he replied. "The body is in exactly the same state as it was when it was brought in to us a few hours ago. No-one has touched it, by police orders."

I drew Holmes' attention to the detail. "Excellent, Watson. I had somewhat suspected that we would find something of the sort. See here." He displayed to me a number of cotton-wool pads which had been found in the dead man's possession. "Not that these are necessarily significant in themselves," he remarked, "but taken in conjunction with this," holding up a small bottle, "I feel that there may be some answer to the problem before us. Note that this pad, especially, has been soaked in liquid at some point in the recent past – the same liquid, I feel certain, that is contained herein."

"What is it?" I asked.

"Precisely what I expected to find," he replied, unstoppering the bottle and holding it under my nose.

"Ether!" I exclaimed. "As we noted in that cellar. But what does it mean? If we had discovered that cotton-wool on the floor, or elsewhere, I would say that Faulkes' assailant had attempted to anaesthetise him. As it is, would he attempt the same on himself?"

"Inhaling or even imbibing ether is popular as a recreation among certain classes of society, it is true," admitted Holmes. "It is possible that Faulkes would have indulged in this way, but I have my doubts as to that. I noticed in the dining-room a goodly supply of fine liqueurs, and those who appreciate good wine and brandy are, in my experience, unlikely to resort to ether as a solace. I may, of course, be wrong, but I feel that I am now close to a solution here. I am confident that the mysterious Signor Paravinci will supply a few of the missing pieces, and then I will be in a position to confirm my suspicions when we return to London."

I must confess that I was completely in the dark. Before we left, I made a sketch of the deceased's ear at Holmes' request, but I could make no sense of his wishes, as indeed, of the whole business, which continued to be a mystery to me.

We returned to the Faulkes residence to find Gregson still seated at the dining table. A young man, by his looks and dress a workman of some kind, was sitting in the corner, flanked on either side by a burly constable.

"Your sense of timing continues to be excellent, Mr Holmes," Gregson greeted us. "Mr Paravinci has arrived not five minutes ago. Sergeant Wilkerson is downstairs with the catalogue, ensuring that the collection is complete and that there is nothing missing." He turned to address the Italian. "We wish to ask you a few questions. First of all, I wish to know whether you are happy for us to speak in English, or whether you wish an interpreter to be provided for you."

"I am happy to speak in English," replied the other, with a very faint foreign accent. "I anticipate no problem in understanding you, and I trust that you will have no difficulty in understanding my replies to you."

"That is a relief," said Gregson. "I dislike working through an interpreter. I must also warn you that this is an official interview, and anything you say will be taken down in writing, and may be used against you in formal criminal proceedings. Is that clear?"

"Perfectly clear," replied the other. "Am I under arrest?"

"No, you are not. You are free to leave at any time, but I have to tell you that this will probably be interpreted as evidence of guilt, and you will then be arrested."

The other shrugged. "I understand."

"Please come here and sit facing us on the other side of the table. I am Inspector Gregson of Scotland Yard, and the gentlemen on my right and left are the private detective Mr Sherlock Holmes and his colleague Dr John Watson who are assisting me."

The Italian stood, and it was obvious that he was a strong, powerfully built young man, who would have had no difficulty in wielding the statue identified as the murder weapon. He had none of the swarthiness we usually associate with the Italian race and indeed, could easily have passed for a certain type of Englishman.

"You are Antonio Paravinci?"

"I am," was the steady reply.

"How long have you lived in England?"

"A little over four years."

"And you have known Mr Faulkes all that time?"

"I have known him since before I arrived in England. Mr Faulkes has been a friend of my family in Italy for many years."

"How do you earn your living?"

Here Holmes interrupted. "My dear Inspector, it is superfluous for you to ask that question. It is obvious that Signor Paravinci earns his living in the printing trade, spending most of his time as a compositor, as is evidenced by his thumb, and the ink under his fingernails."

Gregson flushed, and the Italian smiled faintly. "Yes, I work at a small printing shop, owned and operated by a fellow Italian," he acknowledged. "Fallini and Company, in Whitechapel. I have been with them since my arrival in this country."

"Did you visit Mr Faulkes regularly?"

"I used to visit him monthly, until just over one month ago, when I started to visit him more frequently."

"Would you explain to us why you changed your habits?"

"I would prefer not to answer that, if you have no objection."

Gregson raised his eyebrows, but continued his questioning. "We have been told that you visited this house last night."

"That is so."

"We were also informed that you and Mr Faulkes engaged in a dispute as you were leaving the house."

"It was more in the nature of a disagreement than a dispute," countered Paravinci.

"And perhaps you would care to tell us of the nature of this disagreement?" suggested Gregson, laying what I felt was an unnecessary emphasis on the last word.

"May I refuse to tell you?"

"If you wish to keep silent on the matter, you may do

so." replied Gregson. "I have no authority to compel you in this matter – as yet. After your disagreement, you left the house?"

"I did," the other replied.

"And then?" Gregson sighed. "I hope that you are aware that you are not being very forthcoming, Mr Paravinci."

"Very well. I will tell you what I did. I left the house and walked to the station. I caught the 9:32 train to Euston. From there, I walked to Euston Square station and took the railway to the Whitechapel station. From there I walked to my lodgings in Greatorex Street. I arrived home between a quarter before eleven and eleven o'clock, I guess."

"Did anyone see you either on your journey home, or when you arrived at your lodgings?"

"I am sorry that I am unable to supply you with an alibi," replied the other calmly. "Of course I saw many people on my journey, but none known to me personally. It is possible, I suppose, that the ticket collector at this station or even at Euston or Whitechapel might remember me, but otherwise, I am unable to provide proof of my actions. May I go now? I have work waiting to be completed."

"I have only a few more questions, and then you will be free to leave. First, what is your relationship with Albert Simpkins, the late Mr Faulkes' servant?"

"I hardly know him. He lets me into the house, he shows me to Mr Faulkes. He has served me with food and drink sometimes. Sometimes he lets me out of the house, sometimes Mr Faulkes performs that office himself. I know nothing of him as a person."

Gregson wrote in his notebook. "Do you know Father Patrick Donahue of Holy Rood Church?"

"I know that he is the priest here, and that Mr Faulkes sometimes mentioned him in conversation."

"I suppose it is useless to ask you to describe the content of your conversations with Mr Faulkes?"

Paravinci smiled. "Not entirely useless, Inspector. As you might imagine, we discussed personal matters that I would sooner not mention here. However, much of our conversation revolved around his collection. My uncles in Rome are art dealers and restorers. It is through his dealings with them that Mr Faulkes became acquainted with my family and with me. Very often I acted as an intermediary in some business dealings when he wished to purchase some item for his collection."

"Did you handle money in connection with these dealings?" asked Gregson.

"Yes, he used to entrust me with the money for the purchases on occasion. I was able to remit the money to my uncles through my employer, Fallini, more easily than Mr Faulkes was able to do himself."

"Did you receive a commission for your services?"

The other flushed. "I did not seek any reward in this regard, but Mr Faulkes insisted that I take something for my trouble. This money I did not keep for myself, but gave to St Anne's church in Whitechapel. The priest there can confirm this. Am I now free to go?"

Gregson sighed again. "You are free to go, Mr Paravinci, if Mr Holmes here has no questions?" Holmes shook his head. "But I would advise you to cooperate a little more freely when you are questioned next time about this matter."

"You think I will be questioned again?"

"I am certain of it. I must ask you to wait here for a few minutes only while I complete my account of this conversation, following which I will ask you to sign it."

"Very well," replied the Italian, somewhat sullenly, crossing his legs and folding his arms as he waited.

After a few minutes of writing, Gregson pushed a few sheets of paper towards Paravinci and proffered a pen. "Please read through this, and place your signature at the bottom of each page to show your agreement of this being a true and accurate account of our conversation."

The other took the papers, and scanned them rapidly, affixing his signature at the bottom of each page before rising to his feet, and pushing the papers back towards Gregson. "I may go now?" he asked once again.

"You may indeed," replied the policeman.

As Paravinci turned to leave, Holmes called to him. "One moment, Signor Paravinci. You may wish to make use of this in the near future." He extended one of his calling cards, engraved with his name and the Baker Street address, on which he had scribbled a few words. "Maybe ten o'clock tomorrow morning would be a convenient time for you to call?"

The other, obviously slightly mystified by this, nodded. "I know something of your name and your reputation. I will endeavour to keep the appointment." He bowed slightly, and left the room.

Gregson regarded Holmes curiously. "The man may be

in the cells by ten o'clock tomorrow," he remarked. "You noticed, I am sure that he signed those papers with his left hand?"

"And the deceased's wound would appear to have been inflicted by another's left hand? Yes, I did notice that detail."

"We know that he regularly handled money, and for all we know, valuable works of art on behalf of the dead man. He is an Italian and a printer by trade. Surely you have not overlooked the connection with the papers received by Faulkes?"

"I have not," replied Holmes, evenly,

"We know that he was a regular visitor, and that by his own admission he was here last night. Simpkins identified him as last night's visitor just before you arrived, by the way."

"And did you observe the reaction of both men when they were brought together?"

"There was little to observe on the part of Paravinci," replied Gregson. "However, I noted an expression that appeared to be almost one of sorrow on Simpkins' face when he was led into the room and confronted the other."

"The case against him does indeed look somewhat strong," commented Holmes.

"I would say it is almost convincing," replied Gregson. "I was close to arresting the man on the spot just now for the murder of Francis Faulkes."

"Then it is a very good thing that you did not," retorted Holmes, "for if you had, you would have been making a blunder of the first order, which would have dealt your career a losing card."

"Come now," exclaimed Gregson. "You cannot believe that he is innocent of the murder of Francis Faulkes?"

"I am convinced of his innocence of that crime," said Holmes. "And I would strongly advise you, for the sake of your future, if for no other reason, to stay your hand for the next twenty-four hours, within which time I am positive that I will be able to convince you, too, that whatever other crimes of which he may be guilty – and I am not as yet convinced of the exact facts concerning those – Antonio Paravinci is innocent of murder."

"We know who killed Francis Faulkes, do we not, and he has just left the room," protested Gregson.

"I believe the killer never left the vault," replied Holmes calmly.

Gregson had just opened his mouth to expostulate, but there was a knock on the door, and a middle-aged man entered the room in answer to Gregson's summons, peering through his thick spectacles. He was shabbily dressed in a tweed suit, and his thinning dark hair was combed over his forehead. "Sergeant Wilkerson," announced Gregson, and proceeded to introduce us. As Gregson had mentioned earlier, it was hard to associate the man's appearance with his profession as a police officer. From his looks, he would have been more at home in a University, or maybe as the curator of a museum.

"Inspector Gregson has already spoken of you," remarked Holmes. "I had no idea until then that the Metropolitan Police Force included such a rara avis in its ranks," he smiled.

"I believe I am unique, at least in this country," replied the other, returning the smile, "though some of the Continental forces employ specialists who perform similar functions to my own. Naturally I have heard of you, Mr Holmes, and you, Dr Watson, and it is a pleasure to make your acquaintance." He spoke in a reedy voice, with a little of the academic specialist about it, matching his appearance.

"How do the contents of the room downstairs tally with the catalogue?" Gregson asked Wilkerson.

"I have been unable to discover any discrepancy. I was able to complete the task speedily, since both the catalogue and the collection are excellently ordered, making the task relatively simple. There is, however, a single point that excited my attention."

"That being?" asked Holmes.

"The catalogue contains not only a full description of the items forming their collection, but also their provenance – in other words, the history of the item before it entered the collection, so far as it can be ascertained – and the price paid for the item. It is with regard to that last that my attention was drawn."

"In what way?" asked Holmes.

"Mr Faulkes has been somewhat rash with regard to the payment for many of the items in the collection, in my opinion. It is impossible to fix the precise value of such items with any degree of exactitude, but by my estimate, some items have been purchased for over twice their true value."

"You say some items?" asked Holmes. "The others were purchased for a fair price, in your opinion?"

"I would say that the prices paid for the other items were reasonable, or even under the price I would expect to see asked for them."

"Could this not simply be a matter of chance?" I enquired. "After all, connoisseurs have been known to be in error regarding these matters, have they not?"

"I would agree that this would seem a likely possibility," agreed the specialist, "were it not for the fact that all these purchases were made from the same dealer in Rome."

"The name of this dealer?" asked Holmes. "I fancy I can guess, but I would appreciate confirmation of the matter."

"Is this really of relevance?" asked Gregson. "I really fail to see how the name of an Italian art dealer can be of interest to us. Well, Wilkerson, indulge Mr Holmes' curiosity."

"The dealers in question are called Paravinci Fratelli – that is in English, the Paravinci Brothers."

Gregson looked stunned. "You were correct in your surmise, Mr Holmes. This definitely does seem of relevance." He noticed Wilkerson's bewilderment, and hastened to explain. "The Italian whom we have just been interviewing is named Paravinci, and informed us in the course of our questioning that his uncles are art dealers. You now inform us that the money paid to these Paravincis was over double what it should have been on a number of occasions. This would seem to be of significance."

"This is merely my opinion, Inspector," replied the other. "It might be that other specialists would interpret the pricing of these *objets* somewhat differently from my estimates."

"I hardly think it would be a significant difference," remarked Holmes. "You are, after all, the James Wilkerson who published that definitive monograph on the varnishes used by Cremona violin makers of the seventeenth century, are you not?"

A faint flush stole to the expert's cheek. "Dear me, I had no idea that my fame had spread so far," he exclaimed. "I suppose you are correct. Others might have opinions that would differ slightly from mine, but I do not think it would be a significant divergence."

"It makes the case against young Paravinci look even more damning, does it not?" Gregson said to us.

"Possibly," replied Holmes, with an abstracted air. "I think that one important fact has been imparted to us just now, though."

"That being?" asked Gregson.

"That there is no discrepancy between the entries in the catalogue and the contents of the vault. I suppose," turning to Wilkerson, "that there is no possibility that any pages of that ledger have been removed?"

"None whatsoever. Mr Faulkes was a very conscientious recorder of his collection. All pages and entries are numbered in sequence, and the removal of a page would be instantly detectable."

"Do you have any knowledge of the statues, one example of which was found near the body?" asked Holmes.

"The catalogue marks them as being late thirteenth or early fourteenth century Milanese. They were probably made to stand inside a church or private chapel, given their relatively fragile nature and the type of colouring used on them."

" Were they purchased from the Paravinci brothers?" asked Gregson.

"As it happens," replied Wilkerson, consulting the ledger, "they were not, and he paid what I would consider to be considerably under the market price for them."

"Thank you, Sergeant, that is all we need from you at the moment, is that not so, Mr Holmes?"

"I agree. But it may be that we will require Mr Wilkerson's talents in the future. For now, I have a few further questions that I would like to ask of Simpkins."

Gregson passed the word for Simpkins to be summoned, and Wilkerson left us. The servant entered a few minutes later.

"I have only a few questions for you," asked Holmes. "Firstly, was Dr Addison usually consulted by Mr Faulkes as his medical adviser?"

"Yes, sir. Dr Addison has been his physician for over fifteen years now."

"Did he ever consult any other doctors?"

"About five or six weeks ago, he went up to London, and he told me that he was going to see another doctor in Harley Street."

"Do you know the doctor's name?" asked Gregson.

"I am sorry, sir. Mr Faulkes did not see fit to give me that information."

Holmes posed the next question. "Can you describe Mr Faulkes' moods? Would you, for example, describe him as being a cheerful man?"

"Up until about a month ago, I would have said that he was cheerful, sir. He was happy, and often smiled and joked about matters with me. But over the past weeks, he seemed to change and become more serious."

"Can you tell us whether this change took place before or after the visit to London that you mentioned earlier?"

"As I recall, sir, this was after the visit to London."

"And what of his habits with regard to eating and drinking?" asked Holmes.

"Again, he used to enjoy his food and drink. I don't want to give the impression that he drank a lot, sir, but he did enjoy his brandy of an evening, and he dearly loved a good beefsteak. But after that trip to London, he went off his food, I'd have to say, sir."

"Did he appear in any way ill, in your opinion?"

"I'm no doctor, sir, but I wouldn't have said so. He was an elderly gentleman, and he wasn't getting any younger, if you take my meaning. None of us is, come to that."

"Quite," replied Holmes, shortly. "I think that answers my questions admirably, thank you, Simpkins."

The servant bowed slightly to Holmes and left us.

"I think, Watson, it is time for us to return to London. Inspector, I think you now have all the facts in your possession. It is up to you to work on them and conclude the solution for yourself. If you would care to call on us tomorrow at about eleven o'clock, I think that we will be able to close this case satisfactorily."

Gregson looked at me and shrugged his shoulders as if questioning me. As for myself, I had no more idea than did Gregson as to the solution of the mystery. I therefore shook my head, and followed Holmes out of the room.

The next morning saw Holmes and myself waiting for Paravinci to show himself at Baker Street. Holmes had been irritatingly silent regarding the events at Watford during our return to London and throughout the previous evening.

As soon as we had finished our breakfast, he slipped out of the house, promising to return before ten o'clock. Sure enough, a little before the appointed hour, he returned, bearing a small portfolio of papers. He regard me with a quizzical expression.

"You are, no doubt, wondering whether Signor Paravinci will grace this room with his presence at ten o'clock?" he asked me.

"I was indeed wondering that," I replied. "How can you be certain that he will make the journey here?"

"I think that the message I wrote on the card will be sufficient inducement to bring him to us." As he spoke, there was a ring at the front door, and I could hear Mrs Hudson admitting a visitor. A minute later, Antonio Paravinci entered.

"I had to come," he started the conversation. "Please explain the message that you wrote on the card you gave me yesterday. 'If you do not come, you will surely be hanged' is not the kind of invitation that I am accustomed to receive. Is my life really in such danger?"

"Signor Paravinci, I do not think you quite comprehend the situation in which you currently find yourself. I will lay certain facts before you in order to make my point clear to you. Mr Faulkes is dead through an act of violence. You visited him on the night he died and you are known to have been with him in the room where his body was found and where we are to assume he met his end. You are known to have had a disagreement with him on that very night. You seem unable to prove that you left his house when you claim to have done. Furthermore, you are known to have been entrusted by him with money, and your uncles' business has received unusually large sums of money from him in the past. The average police detective would have no problem in putting these matters together and assuming your guilt. And Inspector Gregson, although his talents are superior to those of most of the detectives employed by the Metropolitan Police, sees no way at present to resolve the issue other than to assume your guilt."

As Holmes continued his recitation, the wretched Paravinci, forced to nod in agreement at every point made by Holmes, grew more and more pale, until I was moved to rise and pour him a glass of water. He accepted it from my hand and sipped gratefully.

"And as a final conclusion," Holmes added, "I am sorry to tell you that my countrymen who would be likely to form the jury in your trial would not look kindly on you, being, as you are, not a native of this country."

"My God!" replied our visitor. "I had not considered matters in the light you have just presented them to me. What am I to do?" he positively wailed.

"You must listen to me, and tell me the truth. I will start by saying that I am positive you did not kill your father."

The effect of these words on the Italian was dramatic. He gave a gurgling cry and pitched forward, the glass of water falling from his hand, and spilling onto the floor.

"Holmes!" I exclaimed. "The man has fainted." I adjusted our visitor's position, and employed the usual methods to revive someone in that condition. The act of loosening his collar and the use of sal volatile soon returned the patient to consciousness. He looked about him wildly, and fixed his stare on Holmes, who continued gazing at him cooly.

"How... How did you know that Francis Faulkes is— was my father?" he stammered. "I will not deny it, since you already appear to have the knowledge."

"By the ears," Holmes replied. "You may not be aware, but the shape of the ear, as I have remarked on other occasions, furnishes an excellent medium for confirming degrees of relationship. Your ear, my dear sir, is of a most distinctive shape, particularly the shape of the lower lobe, and the antitragus. I have only observed that particular configuration once or twice in the past, the most recent occasion being when I examined the body of Mr Francis Faulkes in the morgue. The similarity was too marked to be a coincidence."

The other ruefully rubbed the organ in question. "I had

no idea I was so distinctive in that regard," he remarked. "What more do you know?"

"I actually know very little as a positive fact, but I can make some guesses, and you may care to confirm them. Indeed, I would strongly recommend that you do confirm them for me, or correct me if perchance I have failed to draw the correct inference. Watson here will tell you that I am not infallible," he smiled, "and I appreciate others setting me on the right track on those occasions, admittedly rare, when I am mistaken." He settled into his chair and continued. "I had guessed before this morning that you were born on the twenty-second day of July in 1873. I am sure that the official records will confirm this."

"You are a true magician, Mr Holmes. You are correct. How do you know this?"

"It took no great skill for me to deduce this fact, given the vault under Mr Faulkes' house and the door to it. Let me continue. My guess is that Mr Faulkes had paid a visit to Italy, specifically to Rome, some time late the previous year. Some nine months earlier, in fact." He paused to let the full meaning of the words sink into the other's consciousness.

"I admit that Francis Faulkes is my natural father," cried the other. "He was visiting Italy when he met my mother, and they loved each other. He would have married her in an instant, but her parents – my grandparents – would not hear of her being married to any but an Italian. They drove her out of the house, shamed by her condition, but her elder brothers, who were at that time starting in business as dealers in antiquities, gave her shelter, and cared for her and her new-born child – myself."

"Could your father not have married your mother after your grandparents' death?" I enquired.

"My mother had been made to swear a solemn oath that she would never contemplate marrying anyone except an Italian man. And my mother is a woman of honour – she would never ever break such a promise. But my father – for I can now acknowledge him as such to you, and I may tell you that it is a blessed relief for me to call him by that name at last – continued to love her, and to look after her and me by sending money from England at regular intervals. He also visited Italy regularly, and let me understand, as soon as I was capable of such understanding, that I was his son, and he regarded me as such in every way, short of marriage to my mother."

"And I take it that the money he paid for the *objets d'art* that he purchased through your uncles was more than the market value for these things, and that the surplus went to you and your mother?" asked Holmes.

"That is it exactly, Mr Holmes. When I was a child, he ensured that I was instructed in the English language, and when I came of age, he made arrangements for me to come to England and work here. My uncles had a friend who was in business here as a printer, and it was with this friend that my father arranged for me to find work. It is a trade that I enjoy, and I consider myself to be skilled at it."

"Indeed you are," smiled Holmes. "I have seen samples of your work."

The other looked puzzled, and Holmes withdrew

several sheets from the portfolio he had brought with him earlier. "_I took the liberty of visiting your employer, Signor Fallini, earlier this morning, and he presented me with these. Here, for example, is a theatre programme where you set the type, printed on some excellent Italian paper from the manufactory of Antodelli e Fratelli. Another excellently produced example of type here, set in Bodoni, this being a restaurant menu. And here is one other example combining the characteristics of the two previous examples – a note from the Paradol Chamber – a proof sheet that I obtained this morning from the pile of waste sheets at Fallini's. It matches this," pulling out the paper that had been given to us a few days before by our clerical visitor. Our visitor turned pasty white, and I feared he was about to lose consciousness again. However, he recovered himself somewhat, and pointing with a trembling hand to the paper, croaked, "How did you obtain that?"

"I see no reason to withhold that information from you," replied Holmes. "It was given to me by Father Patrick Donahue of Holy Rood Church, and it was given to him for examination by your father. Rest assured that, to the best of my knowledge, the seal of the confessional has not been broken. Father Donahue was rightly concerned about these notes, and consulted me, bringing this as an example. You are not going to deny that you are responsible for this and the other notes from this supposed source?"

"No, I cannot and will not deny it. I produced all of these, at my father's request."

"Your father requested you to produce printed notes

that threatened his life?" I began, but Holmes checked my enquiry with a waved hand.

"Yes, he did," replied Paravinci, answering my question.

"I think I know why he did this," said Holmes, "and I believe that the subject may be too painful for you to expound. I will, as before, proceed to lay my conclusions before you, and you should confirm or deny the truth of them." The other nodded his head "A little over a month ago, Mr Faulkes consulted a Harley Street specialist, and received the worst news possible. He had not long to live, and the disease which was slowly consuming him would be hideously painful in its later stages."

"You are correct."

"He confided in no-one except his son, and the frequency of your visits to him increased, as a result of your filial devotion to him." He paused, and the other nodded. "Now we come to the most painful part of the story. Mr Faulkes was reluctant, most understandably, to endure the suffering that accompanies his disease, and accordingly determined to do away with himself. As a good Catholic, though, he knew that this was a sin, but he did not inform his priest directly of his intentions, though he did confide in you. I believe, though, that he may have talked with Father Donahue regarding his fears and his despair."

"You are correct so far."

"I believe that one reason why he did not tell Father Donahue of his suicidal intentions was that he intended to leave at least part of his wealth to the Church. Naturally, I am aware that the Church of Rome regards self-murder as a sin. Had he died by his own hand, the Church would not have found it possible to accept his bequest in good faith. Am I correct there?"

"I believe that to be the case, though I hardly consider myself to be an expert in such matters."

"It was therefore necessary for him, if he were to carry out his intention, of making his suicide appear to be either accidental or murder. I assume that you or he, or possibly the two of you together, decided on the appearance of murder, as a seeming accidental death might well have resulted in a post-mortem examination of the body, revealing traces of poison, or whatever method he had elected to take his life. A supposed murder would point to an obvious cause of death, and divert attention away from the idea of his having taken his own life."

"That is so. He felt that if the ground was prepared for a supposed murder, by means of hints dropped to others, such as the priest, and seeming evidence such as the 'Paradol Chamber' notes, his death, though mysterious in some ways, would not be wholly unexpected."

"Surely, though, you must have realised that your involvement in the scheme would place you in some jeopardy? As I said earlier, you were close – indeed, you still are close – to being measured for the hangman's noose."

"I honestly had no idea that the circumstances would place me under such suspicion. I merely wanted to assist my father, who throughout my life had been the best of fathers, given the strange circumstances. I felt I could do no less for him."

"Can you remember the nature of the final disagreement that you had with him? Simpkins claims that he heard you and your father in disagreement before you left the house, if you recall. How much of all of this is known to Simpkins, by the way?"

"Simpkins had been informed by my father of the relationship between him and myself. It was never mentioned by him to me, or me to him, though he sometimes gave me some sign through his eyes or his actions that he recognised the fact. As to the disagreement, of course I remember it perfectly. It was the last time I saw my father. He was complaining of the growing pain, which burned inside him. He said it was becoming intolerable and he wished to end it as soon as possible. I attempted to dissuade him from sudden action, but his mind was made up. I wanted him to remain with us a few days longer, but I could not change his mind." Here the young man began to sob, obviously deeply affected by the recollection of that evening. Through his tears, he continued, "We went outside, and we embraced – for the last time. I knew it was the last time, and my eyes filled with tears, as they do now. How I made my way back to London, I know not. Excuse me." He pulled out a large handkerchief, and mopped his eyes with it.

"There is nothing to excuse," said Holmes, in a kindly tone of voice. "Your display of filial affection is commendable, and I do not see that you could have done anything other than what you did, under the circumstances. Did you know the method by which your father planned to make away with himself?"

The other nodded. "To my shame, I confess that it was of my devising."

"The ventilator cord looped around the arm of one of the statues and swung as a pendulum, with the result that when the stone base hit a solid object, the arm would break away and the statue would slip out of the noose, leaving the impression that the statue had been used as a weapon by the murderer, and had broken on impact. I observed that the statue that actually killed your father was not the first one on which he, or you, had made the experiment."

"How did you deduce all this?" I asked, unable to contain myself.

"It was obvious, Watson," replied Holmes, a little testily. "The arm had detached from the statue. There was no doubt in my mind that the base of the statue inflicted the wound that led to Faulkes' death. From the bloodstains, it was obvious that the arm had become detached following the impact with the body and not before. Forgive the graphic nature of the description, Signor Paravinci, but it was obvious that blood had immediately spurted from the wound with some force, and the arm had landed over some of the blood on the floor. There were only two ways for the arm to have become detached in that way. First, the blow could have been delivered with the arm, but this was obviously not the case. All the signs pointed to the heavy stone base of the statue as being the cause of death. The other way the arm could have been broken off the body would have been if it had been used as the handle of the weapon. You saw me pick up one of those statues. It would have been folly for me to grasp it by the arm. The only logical way to grasp it would have been by the torso."

"I am astounded," said our visitor. "How did you come to the conclusion that you did?"

"Once I had worked out that the arm had broken following the blow administered to your father, it was a matter of calculating out the relative angles of the arm and the rest of the statue, when compared to those of the body and the ventilator cord. My deduction is that the statue was set swinging as a pendulum and pushed to increase the amplitude of the swing, and hence the force with which the statue would strike. When your father judged that the statue was ready to do its work, he could then determine the position where he should stand to await the fatal blow."

I shuddered. "That must have demanded a high degree of courage." I could see in my mind's eye the dying man standing calmly, willing himself not to flinch as the deadly angel swung inexorably towards his head. I noticed Paravinci making the sign of the Cross, his eyes closed, and his lips moving as if in silent prayer.

"Hence the ether," explained Holmes. "I believe, Signor Paravinci, that your father inhaled some ether from a cotton-wool pad before committing himself to his final course of action. This would act as an anaesthetic and help to deaden any pain, as well as dulling his sensibilities. If it is of any comfort to you, I am sure that he felt little or no pain, and we know that his death followed very soon after he had been struck down, and while he was unconscious. I do not believe he suffered. The position and angle of the wound indicate that your father seemed to deliberately position himself to achieve that effect."

"It is some comfort," replied the other. "Do you believe

I committed a sin by aiding him? It is I, after all, who was responsible for setting up the whole business. We tested the idea using some of the other statues, and I fear we broke some of them in our experiments, as you noticed. I cannot help feeling that I have committed a mortal sin in helping my father escape his torment, and that I must be tormented in my turn after my own death."

"These matters are outside my province, I fear," said Holmes gravely. "You must seek that answer elsewhere. As to whether you have committed a crime, I fear the answer to that is in the affirmative. The exact charge would be a matter for the police, but it would not be murder. As to whether you should be tried and convicted for what you did, I cannot, having heard your story, believe that you should suffer the rigours of the law."

"Thank you, Mr Holmes," replied the other.

"Do not be too hasty, however," replied my friend. "I am a private citizen – I am not the representative of the law, and I have no power to bind or loose. Inspector Gregson will be here shortly, and I promise you that I will do what I can to assist you by putting your case before him."

"Why, I thank you, Mr Holmes," replied the other.

"You strike me as a well-mannered and well-meaning young man. I think your conscience will have more effect on your future life and conduct than any legal proceedings could ever do. I have no wish to see you imprisoned for what, in many ways, may be regarded as an act of mercy. I have one more question before Gregson arrives. What was the source of the name of the Paradol Chamber? Was this your doing?"

"My father allowed me to choose the wording and the signatory of the supposed threatening notes. I selected the name myself – with the first part of the name being the first part of my own name, but also meaning 'against' or 'preventative', as in the word 'parasol' and so on. The second part I concocted myself, from the Latin for pain or grief or suffering, 'dolor'. And the Chamber referred to the underground vault. I felt that there was some sort of mysterious sound there that would impress and baffle."

"You were perfectly right," said Holmes. "And here, on cue, is Inspector Gregson."

The policeman entered the room. "Antonio Paravinci," he intoned, on sighting our visitor. "I must ask you to accompany me to the station to answer further questions regarding the death of Mr Francis Faulkes of Watford."

"Are you arresting my client?" Holmes asked.

"At this stage, I am not," replied Gregson.

"In which case, may I suggest, my dear Inspector, that you make yourself comfortable in that chair there, and listen to the story I have to tell you. I take it you have some time to spare?"

"Since it is you, Mr Holmes, I will listen."

"Thank you. A cigar?" Gregson accepted the proffered article, and settled back in the chair while Holmes outlined the facts as he had deduced them and as they had been confirmed by Antonio Paravinci. Occasionally Gregson interjected to confirm the truth of Holmes' narrative with Paravinci.

At the end of this speech, the police inspector sat in silence, finishing the cigar, and obviously lost in thought.

Neither Holmes nor I moved a muscle to disturb him, and Paravinci for his part was on the edge of his seat, biting his lower lip, with his body tensed.

After about five minutes of this, Gregson rose to his feet, and clapped the flinching Paravinci on the shoulder. "Look here, my lad," he said. "You've not been in trouble with the law before this, I know that. We've talked to your employers, and they say you're a good worker. You've been a good son, too, to both your mother, and in your way you've been a good son to your father as well. Mr Holmes doesn't make many mistakes, and if he says this is what has happened, and you back him up on this, I believe him, and you. Now listen carefully to me. There's something very interesting going on on the other side of the road, and I'm going to look out of the window at it. It looks so interesting that if you were to slip downstairs, and catch the next boat train to take you out of this country as quickly as possible, I probably wouldn't even notice you leaving. Do you take my meaning?" Paravinci nodded silently. Gregson turned to Holmes and me. "Dr Watson, Mr Holmes, could you give me your opinions, please?" He pointed out of the window at some unsuspecting coal-heaver. As Holmes and I rose to our feet to join him, I saw Holmes mouth the words "Go now" to our visitor.

The three of us stood side by side, our backs to the room. Not until a full minute had passed after we had heard the door opening and closing did Gregson turn round.

He let out a deep breath. "It would have gone hard

on him had I arrested him. He deserves better," he said simply and without emotion.

"Amen to that," I replied.

"Never fear," chuckled Holmes. "I warrant that Watson will never tell this tale to the public, and that Inspector Tobias Gregson will retain his fearless stony-hearted reputation among London criminals. Another cigar, Inspector, before you return to Scotland Yard and tell the sad tale of how the criminal slipped through the net before your arrival here?"

Sherlock Holmes & The Giant Rat of Sumatra

Editor's Notes

This tale is another of those that Watson chose to bury in the obscurity of the deed box for reasons of discretion. It appears, furthermore, that he also banished much of it from his memory, as his reference to it in The Sussex Vampire has Holmes reminding him that "Matilda Briggs was not the name of a young woman, Watson ... It was a ship which is associated with the giant rat of Sumatra".

The reference to HMS Daring as the fastest ship afloat places the timing of the story at 1895 or thereabouts. This would coincide with the term of The Earl Spencer as the First Lord of the Admiralty who served in that capacity until 1895, replaced by George Goschen. However, it would be foolish to speculate too closely as to the identity of the character referred to as "Lord Haughton", which is an obvious pseudonym, and it is quite likely that Watson deliberately threw sand in the eyes of the readers of this tale as regards the location of "Haughton"'s ancestral seat, etc. We can only guess at the true identity of the other actors in this drama: Captain Frederick Glover, and Senior Lieutenant Ramsay Moffut. Though HMS Bellorophon and HMS Colossus were indeed capital ships in the Royal Navy in the periods mentioned, no officers of the names given here are present in the Navy List of that time associated with these ships, and reports of incidents such as those described are to be found in no official records.

SHERLOCK HOLMES WAS FAR FROM BEING A MODEST MAN, and was proud, with some justification, it must be admitted, of his successes. Even given this, there were several cases where his powerful intellect and energy achieved a solution to a problem that was denied to the official forces, but which he resolutely refused to make known to the public.

In many instances this was the result of what he termed "trivia" – though the case had presented apparently insurmountable problems to our friends at Scotland Yard, Holmes' keen brain had cut through the Gordian knot in an instant, and had presented the police detectives with the answer to the conundrum that had been baffling them, often for weeks. These cases he deemed of insufficient interest to excite readers, though to me these exhibited his extraordinary powers to the fullest.

Other cases demanded discretion as regards their publicity. Several of these have been published, albeit using pseudonyms. Those, for example, who seek the monarch of Bohemia, or even the name of the fair adventuress to whom the King of that fictional realm (fictional, that is, at the time of the events described) was attached, Irene Adler, will seek in vain. I have drawn the veil of decency over the true identity of the European ruler to whom Holmes rendered his services. Nonetheless, the essential facts of the matter are as I have described them, as they are in other such cases.

A third class of case where Holmes desired my reticence concerns those matters relating to the safety and security of the realm. Though he refused any honours such as a knighthood or other rank, Sherlock Holmes was well deserving of such recognition, owing to the numerous occasions on which he served his country, usually for no reward. In a number of these, he worked as a direct agent of the rulers of this nation, and in others, his brother Mycroft acted as the conduit between the detective and those holding high office. It was one of these latter that formed the events that I shall refer to as the case of the "Giant Rat of Sumatra".

Holmes had recently returned from a visit to the Continent, where, he informed me later, he had been assisting the *Sûreté Nationale* of France in their capture of the notorious forger and confidence trickster who had been passing himself off with considerable success as Baron Lemaître. My practice was doing well, and I have to confess that it was with more than a little irritation that I opened a telegram from my friend, which read, "Come at once. Your assistance required urgently."

"I really cannot spare the time," I said to my wife. "Mrs Anderson's case of shingles is coming to a point where I really fear to leave her unattended, and the whole of the junior portion of the Prout family is suffering from whooping cough."

My dear Mary was completely undeceived by my protestations. "John," she told me. "Your patients are not suffering from serious conditions, I am sure. And I know how much you have missed your friend, however much you may deny it. It will do you good to go off with him on one of your adventures. Simply make your usual arrangements with Anstruther to take over for a few days."

It was true; although I was more than content with my lot as a happily married general practitioner, there was a part of my life that I had come to expect from my association with Holmes that was now missing. As is so common, a woman's intuition came closer to the truth than it was possible for mere male rational thought to achieve, and I accordingly made the arrangements as Mary had suggested.

An hour later, I was climbing the stairs to my friend's lodgings in Baker Street, having telegraphed my acceptance of Holmes' invitation, and entering the well-known room where I had spent so many hours in the past. I cast my eye about the apartment for evidence of change, but much seemed as it always had done in the past – the jack-knife skewering the unanswered correspondence to the mantle-shelf, the Persian slipper containing the rough shag tobacco with which Holmes was accustomed to fill his pipe, and the wall above the fireplace where Holmes had patriotically delineated the initials of our Sovereign with bullets fired from his revolver.

Holmes himself was standing in the centre of the room, coated and gloved, hat in hand, apparently impatient to leave. "Come, Watson," he said, pulling out his watch. "We must make haste."

"Where are we going?" I asked as we made our way downstairs and passed into the street.

"The Diogenes Club," replied

"Brother Mycroft?" I asked, having been previously acquainted with Holmes' elder brother and the strange circles in which he moved.

Holmes nodded. "He wishes us to run around on his behalf, or rather on behalf of the government. As you are aware, Mycroft is by no means the most energetic of individuals and he makes use of my energy where he cannot summon up his own."

"You mean that he wishes you to run around on his behalf?" I corrected, placing a slight emphasis on the pronoun.

"You do yourself a disservice, Watson," replied my friend. "I made a specific request for you to be included in the invitation and I will require your assistance, I am convinced. Mycroft has already informed me that the case is peculiarly baffling to him, and if he finds it so, we can be sure that it will be taxing. I need my Watson beside me."

I was under few illusions that my intellect and powers of deduction were in any way equal to those of Sherlock Holmes or his brother, but knew from past experience that my participation would be chiefly as a sounding-board for the music of Holmes' thoughts, though he was kind enough to say otherwise much of the time.

On arrival at the Diogenes Club, that singular establishment where conversation between members is not only discouraged, but forbidden on pain of expulsion after the third offence, we were shown by a porter into the Strangers' Room, the only location within the Club where Mycroft could converse with us without incurring the wrath of the governing committee.

Holmes and I settled ourselves into the comfortable chairs that the Diogenes provides for visitors and awaited the arrival of the elder Holmes. After a few minutes, the massive bulk of Mycroft Holmes blocked the door, which he pulled to before sinking into another chair, which obviously by its size, if not for his use alone, was reserved for those of similar build.

"Well, Sherlock," he greeted his younger brother familiarly. "I see from the press that you have been busy. I take it that the wife in the Fromalle affair had no knowledge that the rubies had been substituted."

"Not until I brought the fact to her attention," replied Sherlock. "I fear that the marriage will end up in the Divorce Court, but it is probably for the best. He is somewhat of a brute, and I fear for her continued sanity if they are to remain together as man and wife."

Needless to say, I had no knowledge of the matter being discussed. As always, I was struck by Mycroft Holmes' considerable intellect, which seemed to provide him with the most intimate details of events, despite his extreme indolence. He and Sherlock debated abstruse points regarding a political scandal in a remote German barony, while I sat astounded at the detailed comprehension displayed by both participants.

"You did not bring us here to gossip about the Graf von Metzelburg, though, Mycroft?" said Homes at length.

"No, the matter on which you and Watson can be of assistance is a good deal closer to home. Dr Watson," he turned to me. "Apologies for not greeting you earlier. I hope that you will serve as somewhat of a brake on my brother's rather wilder extravagant notions. Your good sense will be of great value here." I felt flattered by these words, but given the extraordinary capabilities of the speaker, and those of his brother, I had serious doubts as to any additional value I was able to bestow. Mycroft addressed us both. "As you know, there is to be a change in the composition of the Cabinet in the near future. One of the alterations will be in the Admiralty, where a new First Lord is to take office. Sir Watkin Goodall has served with distinction over the past years, but the Prime Minister agrees with my suggestion that new blood is required there. The nation at this time needs a First Lord who is able to see past the pipe-clay and brass polish and paint, and consider the strength of the Navy in comparison to those navies of our continental neighbours, not to mention those of the United States of America and even of Japan, and take advantage of the new technical developments that are revolutionising the art of naval warfare."

"I am sure when you made this suggestion to the Prime Minister you had a particular individual in mind," Sherlock Holmes remarked.

"I did indeed. Augustus Wilmott, Lord Haughton, the eldest son of the Earl of Harrogate, was the candidate I recommended for the post. He has served with distinction as an officer in the Mediterranean Fleet, and rose to the rank of Captain through his abilities, rather than by reason of his birth. He has a sound practical knowledge of the workings of the Navy at sea, and on his recent retirement from the Service became a director of the firm of naval architects responsible for the design of the latest class of battleships. He is also, as I am sure you are aware, an active Member of the House of Commons. I can think of no better man in the land to step into the shoes of Sir Watkin."

"But there is a problem?" suggested Holmes.

"There is indeed. Lord Haughton has not been seen for the past five weeks at the least."

"He is up in Scotland, killing defenceless animals, or tormenting fish with artificial flies," Holmes replied. "You would not expect to see him in London at this time of year, surely?"

"Sherlock, there are times when I despair of you," retorted his brother. "Do you think that was not the first possibility that suggested itself to me? I have made discreet enquiries among his friends and relatives. None has seen him, received any communication from him or heard word from him over the period I mentioned."

"It would seem impossible for a man of his fame and distinction simply to vanish from view in this way," I broke in. "Surely he must have travelled overseas?"

"Our agents have scoured Europe," replied Mycroft, "and have failed to discover any trace of Lord Haughton in any of the resorts he is known to have frequented."

"Perhaps he has suffered a fatal accident in some remote spot in the countryside and is no more?" I suggested. "This is why he is not to be found anywhere you have searched."

Mycroft Holmes turned his lazy gaze upon me. "For reasons I shall go into later, we believe that this is not the case."

"Do you suspect foul play?" interjected Sherlock.

"With the information available to us at present, we

have no positive evidence one way or the other, but the answer to your question regarding suspicion is in the affirmative. Maybe I should outline the case as we have it so far," suggested his brother.

"Pray do so." Sherlock Holmes and I settled back in our chairs, and I brought out my notebook and proceeded to take notes as Mycroft Holmes explained the matter in his usual logical and incisive fashion.

The facts of the matter as he related them were as follows. Five weeks ago, Lord Haughton had been staying at his father's country residence in Hampshire. He had announced his intention to visit former naval comrades in Portsmouth for a luncheon to be given in his honour, and set off alone for the local station at Shawford from where he would catch the train to Portsmouth. The Shawford station-master, to whom Lord Haughton was well known, had noticed him board the Portsmouth train, and a man answering to his description appeared to have been seen at Portsmouth station. However, in the short journey between the railway station and the battleship HMS *Colossus*, in the wardroom of which he was expected as a guest, he seems to have disappeared.

One of the officers on board the *Colossus* watching through field-glasses claimed to have seen a man whom he took to be Lord Haughton on the quay, boarding a small steam-launch, accompanied by two men whom he did not recognise. It was expected that the steam-launch would then bring him on board the battleship, but instead, it steered towards for a small tramp steamer, passing behind the hull of the latter, and obscuring any view of any passengers disembarking or embarking. The *Colossus'* officer watched the steam-launch return to the quay and dock, but saw no-one resembling Lord Haughton leave the boat, though the two men who had accompanied him on board disembarked and walked together in the general direction of the centre of the town. About ten minutes after the launch had left the coaster, the latter raised anchor and left the harbour. Though the officer reported the incident to his brother officers after the ship had left harbour, it proved impossible to identify the steamer, and since there had been no positive identification of the mystery passenger, it was impossible to persuade the authorities to follow the ship.

The officer, when questioned further, claimed that he could not be absolutely positive that the person he had seen was indeed Lord Haughton, but since he was well acquainted with him, it was considered that his testimony could be relied upon. As to the ship that had presumably carried the passenger away, he was able to give a reasonably detailed description, but it seemed that she had not called at any British ports. He had noticed, however, that the coaster was flying a Dutch flag.

"That would seem to argue that he is on the Continent, as Watson suggested just now," Sherlock pointed out to Mycroft.

"If he is, then he is in some sort of captivity," replied Mycroft. "But we have good reason to believe that he was in this country for some time, even if he has recently been taken to the Continent."

"Your reasons for believing this?"

"The Admiralty have received letters from him, postmarked in this country. One each day, with the series coming to an end a few days ago. It is this sudden cessation that has brought me to your door, figuratively speaking."

"The letters prove nothing," remarked my friend. "Letters can be written in one country and posted in another."

"The handwritten letters all contained references to the newspapers of the morning of the day that the letters were written and posted," remarked his brother, a little testily. "It would not have been possible for those letters to have been written in another country and posted in a British post office box at the time given. All the rules of logic make it certain that he has been in this country up to four days ago. He may still be here."

"From anyone else I would doubt the accuracy of that statement, but from you I will accept that this is in fact the case," said Holmes. "I assume that you have made extensive checks on the authenticity of the handwriting?"

"There can be no doubt as to that," replied Mycroft. "The finest analysts have examined these letters closely, and compared them with confirmed samples of the missing man's handwriting. They are in unanimous agreement as to the fact that these letters could not have been written by anyone other than Lord Haughton."

"And the content?"

"This is another puzzle. There is little of import in these letters. They appear to be no more than ramblings about his health or the weather or the scenery. I have had photographic copies made, which I will have delivered to you at Baker Street. The originals must, as you appreciate, remain in Whitehall."

"There is no secret writing or invisible ink?" asked Holmes.

"Sherlock, I believed you had a higher opinion of my abilities than to ask such a question. And to anticipate the next question I believe you will ask me, no, we have examined the content of these messages for a code or a cypher, but have been unable to find any such."

"Are the police involved in the search?"

"At this stage, they have been given the description of Lord Haughton, but not his name. If they discover a man who answers to the description, they are to inform London immediately. This is to prevent any possibility of panic. The possible abduction of such a prominent member of society would undoubtedly cause considerable public alarm."

"Undoubtedly," Holmes agreed. "How long has the search been proceeding?"

"Just over four weeks."

"And all that has been received in this time are these letters?"

"There was a report last week from the local police that a man resembling Lord Haughton had been seen in Nuneaton. It turned out to be mistaken."

"And I assume you are tending to the conclusion that he has been abducted by agents of a foreign power?" Mycroft nodded his great head silently in answer to his brother's question. "Are there any good reasons why he should be so abducted that you are at liberty to vouchsafe to us?"

"He has been a serving naval officer on many of Her Majesty's most advanced warships of the day. He is intimately involved in the design and construction of the most modern and deadly of the Royal Navy's ships, as well as serving on various Parliamentary Committees concerned with naval affairs. You would be pressed to find one man who knows more about the operation and design of the ships, as well as the political matters concerned with the modern Navy. That, of course, is the reason why I passed along the recommendation that he become First Lord."

"You should have consulted me earlier, Mycroft. You have wasted valuable time." Holmes spoke sternly in a tone of voice I had never previously heard him use to his brother.

"I admit it, Sherlock. But I was given to understand that you had other matters requiring your attention."

"True," replied my friend, "but you know well that you can always call on me in an emergency of this kind. If I am to assist you in this matter, I will require the loan of the originals of the letters, together with their envelopes, as well as photographic copies for me to retain. A copy of the statement of Lord Haughton's brother officer who claimed to recognise him would also be invaluable. I trust you can arrange that, together with a suitable laissez-passer, to open doors that might otherwise remain shut to us?"

"I can certainly have all of that prepared for you."

"Please have them delivered to Baker Street within the morning, together with any likenesses of Lord Haughton that you may have. Watson and I will await these documents, and lay our plans accordingly."

"Well, Watson, a pretty puzzle, is it not?" remarked Holmes as we drove back to Baker Street. "Such an individual typically does not vanish from view unless he has a good reason to remove himself from the public gaze, or unless another party wishes him to be so out of the limelight. The fact that he was escorted to the strange ship and never returned from there, while his companions did so would seem to argue that he was in some way kidnaped or otherwise abducted."

"There is no definite proof of this, if I understood your brother's account correctly," I pointed out. "The officer who described the incident may well have been mistaken, both in his identification of Lord Haughton, and in his description of the events he described."

"And even given that he may have been correct on both those counts, his listeners, including us, may well have been mistaken in our interpretations of those events," added Holmes. "We will have to investigate the events at Portsmouth and discover more. For now," he commented as we arrived at his Baker Street lodgings, "we should examine what Brother Mycroft will send us."

We waited for the promised materials in Holmes' rooms, using the time by verifying details of Lord Haughton's life as recorded in the various reference works filling Holmes' shelves. As Mycroft had informed us, he appeared to be one of the foremost men of the nation in the field of naval affairs. He had served with distinction in ships around the world, including several incidents in the East Indies where he had been decorated for his gallantry, and had commanded several capital ships before retiring from the Navy. His work with the world-renowned firm of naval architects that bore his name had resulted in a stream of orders from overseas as well as from our own Senior Service, and his speeches and statements in Parliament displayed an uncommon grasp of the practicalities of statecraft as it related to naval affairs. Truly, as Mycroft had said, if there were one man who embodied the British naval tradition, it was Lord Albert Haughton.

Our research activities were broken into by Mrs Hudson, who attracted our attention with a knock on the door and a call of "Mr Holmes! Mr Holmes!".

On my opening the door to enquire the reason for her knock, given that she usually directed his clients directly to Holmes' rooms, the landlady appeared flustered. "Begging your pardon, sir," she exclaimed. "I am now accustomed to the police tramping in and out of the house, but this is something else. I'm sure that everything is in order, but it's not what I'm used to."

"What is it, Mrs Hudson?" I enquired. "Is something wrong?"

"It's these soldiers," replied our worthy landlady. "There are three of them with a big box, and they are demanding to see Mr Holmes. There's nothing wrong, is there?" she enquired anxiously.

"Nothing at all," I reassured her. "Please send them up."

The three servicemen, when they appeared at the head of the stairs, turned out to be Royal Marines rather than soldiers; a pardonable mistake from one not well acquainted with military matters. Two Marines carried a stout metal box between them, following their Sergeant, who introduced himself to Holmes.

"Begging your pardon, sir, but our orders were to stay in the room while you examined the originals of these documents we've brought with us. We are then to return them to the Admiralty, leaving you with the copies. Is that clear, sir? If so, sir, I will require your signature on this," producing a sheet of paper.

"I understand, Sergeant," replied Holmes, signing the paper placed before him. "Brother Mycroft seems to be a touch concerned about this business, would you not agree?" turning to me.

"It would seem he has more than a little justification for being so, if what we were told earlier is correct," I replied.

The sergeant ceremoniously produced a key from an inside pocket of his tunic, and used it to unlock the box, which he then opened, revealing the promised documents. Holmes scrutinised both the letters and the envelopes in which they had been dispatched, holding them carefully by the edges, and peering at them through a powerful magnifying lens. "Little of interest," he said, with an air of resignation, "at least, as far as the actual paper is concerned. All of these are the same paper and envelope. The writing is likewise consistently from the same hand, and the same pen and ink have been used to write every one of these, including the address. There is one point in common, though, regarding the envelopes. I doubt very much whether Mycroft failed to remark the fact, but he omitted to mention it to us. Look here. These are the envelopes of these epistles, arranged in the order of their posting. Observe the postmarks."

I accepted the glass from Holmes and bent over the papers in question. "These are all ports," I remarked. "And the order would seem to indicate a slow trip from Portsmouth along the south coast towards the east of the country."

"Indeed. And that indicates?"

"That the writer was on board a ship or a boat travelling to the last port mentioned, Gravesend, from which he might have travelled to the Continent, I guess."

"I concur," replied Holmes. "The ship in question was obviously taking its time. Indeed, if you look here," and he pointed to a group of envelopes in the series, "the ship actually doubled back on its course at this point. Obviously it was in no hurry to reach its destination. However, it should be a simple matter to search the records of the ports along the coast, and discover those ships that entered and left harbour on these dates. I am certain that we can then make a unique identification of the ship in question. The question then arises in my mind as to why Mycroft has not informed us of the results of such an enquiry, assuming that such was carried out."

"Maybe because he did not want to arouse suspicion as the result of an official investigation?" I suggested.

"That is possible," conceded my friend. "In any event, I feel I have gained all that I can from these original documents, and they can be returned to the Admiralty."

The Marines returned the documents to the box in which they had been transported, and locked it.

"And now," said Holmes, as the box's escorts made their way noisily down the stairs, and found their way to the street, "we travel to Portsmouth."

Holmes was silent during the journey to Portsmouth, and I likewise refrained from making conversation, occupying my time by studying the copies of the documents that had been entrusted to us by Mycroft.

The report of the *Colossus* officer was much as Mycroft Holmes had described, and I could gain nothing fresh from its study. The content of the letters was unremarkable, verging on the trivial. They provided little information, and indeed were almost childish in their composition. Indeed, it was hard to see why they had been written, other than to provide a kind of reassurance as to the writer's very existence. As Mycroft had observed, each letter contained a reference to a topical event, which I assumed had been reported in the national press only on the day when the letter was posted.

The first letter began as follows, "Read this, and know that I am well, though living under strange conditions that I am not at liberty to disclose." It continued in the same vein for a mere two or three sentences, referring to a speech made in the House of Commons late the previous evening, and I turned to the next epistle.

"As I mentioned in my last letter, I am still in good health. I am unaware of my current whereabouts, but may assure you that I continue well." Again, the same trite style, with a reference to recent Parliamentary affairs. I sighed, and turned to the next.

This started, "My health continues to be good, and I am in comfortable surroundings." By this time I had almost given up any hope of making any sense of them, and in the last letter that I troubled myself to read, being the fourth of the series, I read, "Some may question the purpose of these letters, but I assure you that they are simply to provide the world with reassurances of my continued health and existence."

Two or three times I was on the verge of asking Holmes for his opinion on the matter, but when I observed him to be apparently lost in deep contemplation, his eyes seemingly closed, I turned back to the documents without a word.

However, as we left the station and proceeded towards the naval harbour, Holmes turned to me, and remarked, "I believe you are correct, Watson. Those letters would seem to have no purpose except to let the recipients know of the continued existence of Lord Haughton."

"How in the world did you know that was the subject of my puzzlement?" I asked, as always amazed by Holmes' apparent ability to read my mind.

He smiled. "It was somewhat obvious, Watson, from my study of your face and actions as you perused those letters. And yet I believe there is something more to them than meets the eye. Naturally, we may assume that they were written under a certain level of duress, at the orders of his captors, but even so... I thank you, by the way, for your continued silence throughout the journey. There are few companions to whom such a gift is given. We will, I think, make straight for the *Colossus*."

"Do you know she is in port?"

"I read in Monday's newspaper that having returned from a patrol in the Bay of Biscay, she had been experiencing boiler trouble and accordingly was expected to be under repair for a week or so."

On attempting to enter the dockyard, a sentry guarding the gates stopped us and demanded to know our business. Upon Holmes producing the document from the Admiralty requesting all whom it might concern to give us all possible assistance, the sentry drew himself up to attention and saluted smartly. I half-started to return the salute before I remembered that I no longer wore the Queen's uniform. Holmes appeared to take the matter in his stride, and demanded of the sentry the route we should follow in order to reach the *Colossus*.

On being directed, we passed through the mass of machinery and supplies needed to maintain the ships defending our nation, losing our way and asking for directions several times as we did so. Eventually we found ourselves at the base of the gangway leading to the *Colossus*, guarded by a Marine sentry, who passed a message to the battleship's Captain when we displayed our Admiralty pass and explained that we wished to interview Sub-Lieutenant Fortescue, who had reported seeing Lord Haughton before his disappearance.

Within a few minutes, we were greeted by a young officer who came down the gangway to meet us.

"The Captain's compliments," he announced, "and he would like to welcome you both on board, gentlemen. Please have the goodness to follow me. Take care as you move around the ship, as some of the spaces are rather low." He led the way through a complex mass of steep ladders and narrow corridors until we reached a stout mahogany door, at which our guide knocked.

We were welcomed into the cabin of Captain Frederick Glover, the very epitome of the bluff weather-beaten English sea-dog, who smiled as he extended a welcoming hand and waved us into chairs by his desk. "The celebrated Sherlock Holmes, upon my life," he greeted my friend. "We have no murders on this ship, you know. I fear your talents will find no outlet here. And Doctor Watson himself. Delighted to make your acquaintance. Now, I was told that you wished to speak with Sub-Lieutenant Fortescue, and you bear important papers from my lords and masters in Whitehall?"

Holmes passed over the document in question, and Captain Glover scanned it in silence. "May I ask whether this is in connection with the disappearance of Lord Haughton?" he asked.

Holmes frowned. "I had been given to understand that this was a confidential matter, sir."

"There are few secrets on board ship, Mr Holmes. I can assure you, though, that outside this ship's wardroom, nothing is known of this matter. It would seem to be a matter of serious concern, then?"

"Indeed so," said Holmes, but would say no more,

despite the obvious wish of Captain Glover to be better informed about the business.

"Very good," replied the officer, after about a minute's silence. "There are obviously wheels within wheels here of which I am not permitted to be aware." His tone was stiff. "I take it you will want to see Lieutenant Fortescue now in private?"

"If you would be so kind as to arrange that," replied Holmes. "I do apologise for the secrecy, but I am sure you comprehend the delicate nature of the situation."

"To be sure," answered the Captain, but to my eye he appeared unconvinced. "I will order the Sub-Lieutenant here, and I am sure that we can arrange suitable privacy for your interview." His tone was still frosty.

As he went to the door to pass along the order for the officer, I leaned over to Holmes and whispered softly to him. "Holmes, I am aware that you dislike this matter of fame and notoriety, but it would behoove you to take the Captain here under your wing, as it were. He has obviously heard of you and your abilities, and he seems excited to have you on board ship as a guest. I am sure he could be of service to us in our investigation were you to attempt to build up a friendship with the Captain. I strongly advise you to flatter the man, and feed his sense of importance. He is, after all, a senior officer in the Service, and can undoubtedly do us a good turn if he is well-disposed towards us."

"Hah!" exclaimed Holmes, almost silently. "You may have hit upon something there." He seemed to relax somewhat in his chair as Captain Glover returned to us.

"Captain," he addressed the skipper, "you mentioned that of course you have no murders aboard the ship. My profession has taken me to many places, but I confess this is my first time aboard one of Her Majesty's ships. I would be obliged if you could enlighten me regarding the crimes that you actually do encounter about this floating village. I am always anxious to extend my knowledge and experience, and who could be better placed to assist me in these matters than yourself?" There could be no-one more charming and ingratiating than Sherlock Holmes when he chose to be so, and he was now at his best as regards these qualities.

"With pleasure," remarked the Captain, and Glover launched with gusto into a series of tales of petty theft, drunkenness, and occasional assault. He concluded with, "But these must be nothing compared to what you have experienced in London, Mr Holmes?"

I was glad to see my friend accept the proffered bait, and he regaled Captain Glover, to the other's obvious pleasure, with a few details of some of our adventures, when a knock on the cabin door interrupted him.

"Enter!" bellowed Captain Glover, in a voice that appeared to have been forged in the days of sail, when it was necessary to call to men working the sails high up on the masts of the ships of that day. A young officer entered. "Sub-Lieutenant Fortescue," the Captain said to him, thankfully in a more normal tone of voice, "these gentlemen here are Mr Sherlock Holmes and Doctor John Watson, and they would like to ask you some questions in private." He turned to us. "I will leave you in this cabin. Please pass the word for me when you are finished, and I hope that you will do me the honour of dining with me and some of my officers later in the day." Obviously Holmes' conversation had worked on him, and softened his mood.

"I hope we will be able to accept your offer," Holmes responded. "Now, Sub-Lieutenant Fortescue," he addressed he officer when the door had closed behind the Captain, "I am making enquiries regarding Lord Haughton. I understand that you believe you saw him, or someone very like him."

"That's true, sir," replied the other, and proceeded to confirm the story that Mycroft Holmes had told us earlier, and the written statement of which we had received.

"You did not recognise the two men who accompanied Lord Haughton to the other boat, and returned without him?" asked Holmes.

"No, sir, I did not."

"And how sure are you that the man you saw was Lord Haughton?"

"I am as sure as I can be, sir. The man certainly had his general appearance, and in addition, limped in a somewhat distinctive fashion, similar to the way in which I had observed Lord Haughton walking when he had visited the ship on previous occasions. He suffers from a curious dragging and twisting inwards of the left foot, only apparent when he walks fast. I have never observed anything similar."

"Was he dressed for travelling, did you notice? Was he carrying any luggage?"

"No luggage, sir, and he was dressed in a frock coat and wearing a silk hat, as I had observed him wear on previous visits."

"Can you describe the ship to which the three men were carried?"

"A coaster, a tramp steamer. Single funnel, black with a red band, flying a Dutch flag, sir. Her hull was," and he closed his eyes as if in thought, "black, and the superstructure was yellow."

"You cannot remember her name at all?" asked Holmes.

"Alas, I was unable to do so, as there was another ship in front of the Dutch ship's bows, blocking the name which would have been painted there."

"I would like you to draw a plan of where you saw this Dutch coaster, if you would," Holmes requested, bringing out his notebook and proffering his pen.

"Let me see," said the other, sketching in a plan of the harbour. "We were at anchor approximately here," marking a point on the map, "and the ship to which he was taken was here," marking another point.

"I see," said my friend, taking the book, and examining the plan. "And you have no recollection of seeing the other two men before?"

"None, sir," replied the young officer.

"Did he appear to be accompanying them voluntarily?" asked Holmes. "Or was there any appearance of coercion?"

"It would be impossible for me to say, sir, from that distance."

"Do you know who invited him to dine on board? Captain Glover, perhaps?"

"That would be Senior Lieutenant Ramsey-Moffat. He had served with Lord Haughton on other ships and is a good personal friend, I believe, and he had invited him as a guest of the wardroom on several previous occasions. He was an excellent mimic, and had a very pleasant voice when he cared to sing." For some reason, the young officer started to laugh quietly to himself, as if remembering some incident. "I apologise, sir," he eventually managed to say. "Rather an amusing incident that took place on one occasion that he was with us. He was ready to sing some popular ditty, when a rat entered the wardroom through one of the ventilators. I have never seen such a reaction from a man in my life. He explained to us, when the rat had been removed by a rating, and he had been persuaded to come down from the table on which he was standing, that he had an irrational fear of mice and rats, which always had a similar effect on him. That notwithstanding, we were always happy when Lieutenant Ramsey-Moffat announced that he would be joining us in the wardroom. Although he had been a Captain in his days of active service, he was always ready to talk with any officer and offer advice and assistance. There was one time when Sub-Lieutenant Urquhart was about to be sued for breach of promise, and Lord Haughton was of great help in the matter. Why, he—"

"I think, maybe, we should have a brief word with this Senior Lieutenant," remarked Holmes, choking off what promised to be a long and irrelevant excursion. "Is there anything else that pertains to the matter at hand that you would like to add before you leave us?"

There was nothing of that nature to add, and Holmes dispatched Sub-Lieutenant Fortescue with instructions to pass the word for Senior Lieutenant Ramsey-Moffat to join us. After about ten minutes, the officer in question was admitted to the cabin. He was a florid middle-aged man, somewhat more portly than I would have expected of a naval officer, and was breathing hard as he took his place facing us across the table.

"I am a busy man, Mr Holmes," were his first words to us.

"So are we all," replied Holmes, evenly. "I will not keep you from your duties for long, I expect. I merely wish to confirm a few facts about Lord Haughton."

"Very well. By the way, I should mention that during the time that Lord Haughton was in the Service, he hardly ever used the courtesy title to which he had the right, and was always addressed by his family name, as Augustus Wilmott."

"May I ask whose invitation was extended to him to dine aboard this ship?" asked Holmes.

"It was mine, sir. I am the only one on board who has served with him previously, and I had invited him to dine on several previous occasions as a guest of the wardroom. He was a popular guest with the officers."

"You had served on ships with him in the past?" asked Holmes.

"Yes, indeed. It seemed that we were fated to serve together on various ships, and as a result, we became good friends."

"Understandably. And in his last post at sea, when he commanded the *Iron Duke*?"

"When he took command of her, I was posted here to the *Colossus*, where I have remained since."

"Very good. I have just been informed that he had suffered from some sort of injury that left him with a limp. Do you know how he came by this? We were also informed that you have served with him in the past, so I consider this to be a fair question," asked Holmes.

The other's already ruddy face flushed a little more. "Is it necessary for you to know this, sir?" he asked.

"The most irrelevant-seeming facts may take on importance in the future. You may rely on my confidence," Holmes assured him. "If the information has to be made public, there is no need for your name to be associated with it. You may speak as freely in front of Watson here as you may myself – Watson is the soul of tact and discretion."

The other spoke, but still with some hesitation. "This is the first time that I have ever told the true story, and I cannot believe that I am telling it to anyone, even now."

"I thank you for the trust you are reposing in us," said Holmes. He sat impassively, his fingers steepled, as the other told his tale.

"It was while we were serving together on the old Billy Ruffian – the *Bellorophon*. We were stationed near the Dutch East Indies. We had put into the port at Jakarta, and all of us – the officers, that is – had shore leave, and we took turns, as is usual, in remaining aboard and manning the ship. The natives would swarm round the boat, and try to climb aboard. We needed to keep constant watch in order to prevent them from boarding and thieving from us. One night it was my turn to keep watch in this fashion – all the other officers were ashore – and I heard one of the boats coming back early. When it got closer, I saw that it was not one of our own boats, but one of those operated by the Dutch port officials. There were several of the Dutch police officers in it, and Augustus Wilmott was lying in the boat, unconscious, with his leg bound up in bandages. The police demanded to talk to the Captain, but he was ashore, of course, and they had to make do with me, a mere junior lieutenant at the time, but it seemed I was good enough for them. Naturally, I was worried about Wilmott, and I asked what had happened, and how he had sustained his injury. It seemed that he had been in a house of very ill repute indeed, where some very vicious practices went on – I will not enlarge on the details." Here the good fellow stopped for a while, obviously embarrassed by the tale he was recounting. "Suffice it to say that they are those practices of which mariners are often accused. Loathsome and disgusting vices. In any case," he went on hurriedly, "it appeared that there had been some heated discussion regarding money, and Wilmott had been involved in some sort of affray. The police had been called, and Wilmott had fled, not unnaturally wishing to escape any scandal. He had tripped on some filth and his ankle was twisted, possibly broken. The police identified him as one if the *Bellerophon*'s crew and brought him to the ship. It seemed that they had no interest in arresting him or taking matters any further – in fact, they seemed keen to keep the whole thing very quiet and not to make any further trouble – but they brought him back to the ship."

"I see," said Holmes. "And you were the only officer on board at the time?"

"I was, and I was therefore able to put about the story that Wilmott had been attacked, and had slipped and broken his ankle – for so later turned out that this was the case – when eluding his pursuers. The event was so written up in the log."

"And I am sure that he was grateful to you for doing this?"

"Yes, he was." He seemed reluctant to discuss this aspect of the matter further, however.

A thought occurred to me, and without thinking, I asked the question that came to my mind. "You were aware that your fellow officer had such, shall we say, predilections," I burst out, "and yet you continued to be friends with him?" I noticed Holmes glance at me, and then look back at the naval officer with intense interest.

Ramsey-Moffat turned an even deeper red. "He explained to me, in strict confidence, that the affairs of that evening were an aberration. Or rather, that they were a mistake. He had entered the wrong house, as it were, being mistaken as to the true nature of the residents there. In any case, he told me that this was the first time in his life that such an incident had occurred, and that such would never happen again." He paused a little. "And to the best of my knowledge, that is the case."

"Thank you, Lieutenant Ramsey-Moffat. I hope we will meet at dinner this evening with Captain Glover."

"Unfortunately, that will not be possible. Duty forbids." He pulled out a large ornate watch and examined it. "And duty calls me now."

"Well, then, I must bid you farewell, it seems, and thank you for your help."

The officer left us, and Holmes turned to me. "I sense trouble here. Deep and dark trouble that bodes ill for the Navy, and even for the safety of the realm."

"Because of one foolish incident some years ago that may have been a ghastly mistake?"

"Indirectly, that might be said to be the case, I suppose. That officer is a plausible liar, though." He sighed.

"Holmes," I exclaimed, somewhat astounded. "Are you insinuating that an officer of the Royal Navy, holding Her Majesty's commission, has been telling us less than the truth?"

Holmes smiled. "I will not say that his testimony to us was a tissue of lies from beginning to end, but I fear it was largely untrue."

"On what do you base this accusation, Holmes?"

"Why, on the man's watch, of course. Or, shall we say, the watch that he pulled out of his pocket. Did you not notice the engraving on it?"

"I failed to do so."

"The initials A.W. cannot under any circumstances be those of Senior Lieutenant Ramsey-Moffat. They could, however be those of a certain other gentleman."

"I cannot conceive of any conclusions you can draw from this."

"I can conceive of too many, Watson, and none of

them is a pleasant one. Let us return the use of the good Captain's cabin to him, and we will spend the day in the town, seeking what information there is to be had here. And I believe we could spend a very profitable evening by accepting Captain Glover's hospitality. What do you say to that?"

"As long as the bill of fare is something other than bully beef and ship's biscuit," I laughed. "Very good. Let us follow your suggestions."

Before we left the ship, we talked to Captain Glover and accepted the invitation. At my urging, Holmes also told him a little more of the case on which we were engaged, while omitting any mention of the story we had been told by his Senior Lieutenant, and swore him to secrecy. As I had expected, the Captain appeared to be impressed by the confidence reposed in him by Holmes, and promised us every assistance in our work.

Holmes was once again pre-occupied as we walked off the ship into the town.

"Watson," he said to me suddenly. "Why in the world would that officer tell us that story with all the details? Why could he not have told us the story he recorded in the log?"

"He wishes to set our minds against the missing man? To prejudice our thoughts against him?"

"That is my feeling. And again, I ask myself why? Does he wish us to continue our enquiries less zealously? If so, he will be sadly disappointed. To every action there is an equal and opposite reaction, and you know well, Watson, that if I am pushed in one direction against my will, I will push back with an opposite force, which will exceed the force with which I am pushed. No, Lieutenant Ramsey-Moffat," he soliloquised, "you make me more, not less, interested in the disappearance of your friend, if friend he truly be."

We walked on until we reached the harbourmaster's office, where Holmes made enquiries as to the identity of the ship that had been described by Fortescue.

"The *Matilda Briggs*, registered in Rotterdam," said Holmes as we emerged from the office. "We now have a name for the ship. It should be easy enough for the Board of Trade to trace her calls at the ports around the coast, and we can then match those to the letters received by the Admiralty. Let us send a cable to the Board of Trade, and ask them to find out more about this ship and where she has berthed recently. Then we will reserve lodgings for the night, as I think we will partake of the *Colossus*' hospitality this evening, but spend the night on shore."

We sent the telegram, requesting that the reply be sent in care of Captain Glover on board the *Colossus*, and Holmes returned to the docks while I booked our accommodation at the George Inn. It had cost Holmes a number of florins to obtain it, but in the end he had a little more information about both the *Matilda Briggs*, and her visit to Portsmouth, as he told me before the fire in the front parlour of the inn.

"A Dutch skipper, and a dusky crew, possibly from the

Indies, by the sound of them," he summarised rubbing his hands together briskly. "With one or two Dutch officers. A cargo of miscellaneous items, including sacks of grain and cheap tinware. I cannot attach any significance to that. It is strange, but no-one had any recollection of any previous visits by the ship. Typically such vessels will follow a fixed pattern, I believe, and it is unusual for them to break their habits in this way."

"What about the men who escorted Lord Haughton to the boat? Did you discover anything?"

"I was fortunate," he replied, "in being able to talk with the very boatman who carried the missing man to the *Matilda Briggs*. He was able to give a full description of the two Dutchman who escorted Haughton. The descriptions meant nothing to me, except that he mentioned that both men were heavily tanned, and spoke very little English. Though they arrived at the boat at the same time as Lord Haughton, it seems that they did not form a party. The boatman was first hired by them to take them to the *Matilda Briggs*, and following that, he was given to understand that he was to carry Lord Haughton to the *Colossus*."

"What actually transpired?"

"According to the boatman, Lord Haughton was forced by his companions to mount the accommodation ladder to the coaster, escorted by them. He was received at the top by two of the native crew, and his two Dutch companions re-joined the smaller boat. They then paid him five pounds to return them straight to the dock, and to say nothing to anyone about the event."

"He told you all," I objected.

Holmes chuckled. "I drew him on a bet. I had gauged him, thanks to the betting slip I observed in his hatband, as a man who was not averse to a wager, and I was right in my assumption. I bet him that he had not carried passengers of more than a dozen nationalities within the past month. I was sure to lose my bet, as I had already counted the flags of fifteen nations on the ships in the harbor. I had to listen to tales of Finns and Swedes and Russians before we came to our Dutchmen, but we arrived there in the end."

"And now?" I asked.

"Now we return to the *Colossus*. I trust that Captain Glover will forgive us for our sins in not dressing for dinner."

The telegram from the Board of Trade was waiting for Holmes when we boarded the *Colossus* and entered the Captain's cabin. "As I thought," said Holmes, tearing it open and scanning the contents. "There is a perfect correspondence between the ports of call of the *Matilda Briggs* and the postmarks of the letters received from Lord Haughton. We can therefore conclude that he was being held on board the ship, and maybe still is on board."

"Where is the last port of call recorded?" I asked.

"Gravesend, a few days ago, which corresponds to the last letter received."

"And you think that she is now in Holland, with Lord Haughton aboard?"

"I believe that is what we are intended to think."

"May I make a suggestion," Captain Glover broke in. "Forgive me, gentlemen, but since you were good enough to take me into your confidence, I have been considering the matter. If you would care to use the facilities available to us, we could send a coded cable to the Admiralty, and the Admiralty agents in Holland and elsewhere on the Continent could investigate the matter and discover the whereabouts and possibly even the intentions of this mysterious Dutch vessel. I confess that I fear for Lord Haughton. Though I am not personally well acquainted with him, he is of course known to me, and he enjoys a sterling reputation among his brother officers, and to see him in Whitehall would be of great advantage to all of us who serve at sea."

"Then let us adopt your excellent suggestion," Holmes said to the Captain, who appeared highly gratified that his idea had been taken up by the famous detective. "Would you have any idea how soon we could expect an answer?"

"Of course, I cannot be sure," replied Glover, "but it seems to me that this is a question that could be solved within twenty-four hours at the very most. You are probably aware that we have agents in every coastal port on the Continent. During the time we await a reply, I would like to extend the hospitality of the Royal Navy to you both."

"Most kind of you," answered Holmes, "but we have reserved rooms at the George, close by the dock." The other's face fell somewhat, as it seemed to me that he was anticipating the cachet of hosting Sherlock Holmes as a guest of the *Colossus*, but his countenance brightened to some extent when Holmes added, "We would, however, welcome the use of a room such as this as a base for our operations while we are in this town."

"Naturally," Glover assured us, the smile returning to his weather-beaten face. "My cabin is your cabin, as the Spaniards almost have it."

"Your cooperation will not go unremarked, I assure you," said Holmes. "Now let us draft this message."

The message was soon written, and passed to the signalman for encoding and transmission over the Admiralty telegraph system.

"And now dinner," invited Captain Glover.

AFTER THE admirable dinner, we returned to the George, despite the Captain's protestations, where we turned in and I, for one, slept soundly.

I was awakened early the next morning by a hammering on my door. On opening my eyes, I perceived that it wanted an hour or more before dawn, and I was somewhat annoyed, if not altogether surprised, by Holmes' voice bidding me to awake and dress myself. I hurriedly prepared myself for the day, omitting my morning shave, there being no hot water, and went downstairs to meet Holmes, who was waiting in the parlour together with a seaman whose cap band read "Colossus".

"I beg your forgiveness for this early call, Watson,"

Holmes apologised to me. "I was myself awakened some time ago by this messenger from the *Colossus*. Captain Glover has received a reply from Whitehall, and requests us to meet him at the dock. It would appear that the game is afoot." Even in the dim morning half-light, I could see that his eyes were positively shining with excitement.

"We are not to meet him on board the *Colossus*?"

"It would appear not."

We hurried through the darkened streets, following our guide, to a part of the dock which we had not visited the previous day. Captain Glover was waiting for us, a broad smile creasing his face.

"I would advise you to don these," he remarked, pointing to two sets of oilskin waterproof clothing, similar to what I now noticed he himself was wearing. "Our vessel today provides less protection against the elements than does the *Colossus*." He gestured to the water below, where a sleek vessel rode the waves. A curiously low and rounded hull gave her the appearance of some sinister sea creature. "Behold Her Majesty's Ship *Daring*, which has been described in the press as 'the fastest ship ever'. She made twenty-eight knots on her trials, approximately thirty-two miles per hour."

"I am puzzled," I said. I admit to having been still somewhat irritated at having been pulled from my warm bed to stand on a cold dockside where a light rain was unmistakably starting to fall, and my tone was somewhat sharp.

"We are on the trail of your quarry," Glover explained. "I received a cable from the Admiralty that the *Matilda*

Briggs had departed Cherbourg last night, giving Southampton as her next port of call. I have therefore commandeered the use of the *Daring* to lie in wait for her and to board her if necessary. The 12-pounder gun should prove a sufficient means of persuasion."

"What manner of ship is this?" I asked, looking down. "She seems to be very long compared to her beam."

"She is a new type of vessel, which we call a 'torpedo boat destroyer', designed for the purpose of protecting the Fleet's capital ships against the menace of the smaller torpedo boats that are now being deployed by navies around the world."

"On this occasion, we do not wish to destroy," remarked Holmes. "But a fast ship of this type will allow us to make an easy rendezvous with a slow steamer such as the *Matilda Briggs*, it is true."

"I have acquainted the *Daring*'s skipper, Lieutenant Fanshawe, with the broad outline of our mission, but no more than that," replied Glover.

"I take it that you will be accompanying us, then?" I asked Captain Glover.

"Naturally," he smiled. "If the life of a fellow officer is at stake, I have no alternative but to assist. In any event, I would not miss such an adventure for the world." I could not help feeling admiration for such a man, who was willing to expose himself to possible danger (for we had no knowledge of the disposition of the crew of the *Matilda Briggs*) in defence of his fellows. Truly, I felt, the safety of the nation was assured if it was in the hands of such as Captain Glover.

We descended to the deck of the *Daring* where we were greeted by the young Lieutenant Fanshawe, whose manner reminded me of some of the younger officers in my Army days whose pleasure seemed to be chiefly derived from exposing themselves to danger, engaging in tiger hunts, pig-sticking, or steeple-chases. It was clear to me that dash and élan of this type would be a positive advantage to the commander of such a speedy and glamorous craft, and though I experienced a little anxiety at the thought of a trip in the *Daring*, I also felt a sense of exhilaration. Holmes appeared to suffer from no such qualms, but boarded the deck of this strange new vessel as if he had been a seaman all his life. Not for the first time I admired his adaptability to strange circumstances.

"I apologize, sir, for the lack of ceremonial in not piping you aboard," the Lieutenant said to Glover, saluting smartly. "I took it, though, that on an occasion like this it would be somewhat superfluous."

"Quite correct, Mr Fanshawe," replied Glover. "This is a slightly irregular proceeding, and I do not feel we should be standing on that kind of ceremony here." He then introduced Holmes and myself to the Lieutenant.

"I am sure that you will have more than enough to do once we are underway, Lieutenant," Holmes said to him, "and we will try to keep ourselves from being underfoot, if you will show us where we can stow ourselves."

"I am sure there is room on the deck," replied the Lieutenant. "Please follow me."

It was a tight fit for the three visitors on the small part of the deck that was unoccupied by machinery, despite the vessel's size. Almost as soon as we had taken our places, the engines started, and we could feel the vibration of the reciprocating engines and the three propellers. We rapidly moved away from the dock, and slipped into the Solent, where we picked up speed. The spray whipped off the wave crests, and I began to appreciate Captain Glover's forethought in the matter of the oilskin waterproof clothing.

Sherlock Holmes stood slightly forward of the Captain and myself, standing on a low platform, his long neck craned forward as he strained his eyes towards the horizon, for all the world like some beast of prey on the track of its quarry.

"When did the *Matilda Briggs* leave Cherbourg, Captain?" Holmes shouted into the wind without turning his head to look round.

"At about ten o'clock last night. We can assume an average speed of no more than nine knots from her, so with a distance of around ninety nautical miles of sailing between the ports, we can expect her to enter the Solent at around eight o'clock – maybe a little before that, should she prove to be faster than our estimate. We have another two hours or so before then."

"That should prove ample in a ship this fast," replied Holmes.

"What," I asked, "if the ship is not going to Southampton after all, but makes for another port?"

"All watchers along the French, Belgian and Dutch coasts, as well as those on the German and Danish ports on this side of the Skagerrak are on the alert," replied

Glover, "as well as a close watch now being kept by all harbourmasters in the United Kingdom."

"I must congratulate you, Captain," Holmes called back to us. "You appear to have sealed every possible exit. I believe you would succeed in my profession were you ever to quit the sea."

The seafarer laughed. "I hardly think so, Mr Holmes. In this case, it was simply a matter of elementary naval tactics." However, I noted that Captain Glover appeared to appreciate these words of praise from Holmes.

"Hard a-port! Hold on to the ship!" the Lieutenant shouted from in front of us, as the ship heeled sharply to port. We were almost flying through the water by this time, and the wind whistled past our ears. Truly, this remarkable vessel deserved the title that it had been awarded by the Press.

Captain Glover pulled his watch out of his pocket and scrutinised it. "We are almost an hour ahead of the timetable we can expect the *Matilda Briggs* to follow," he observed. "We can afford a little time for relaxation, I would think."

As if on cue, the rumble of the engines lessened, and our speed in the water dropped to something more closely resembling my conception of a normal ship's speed.

"Breakfast?" shouted Lieutenant Fanshawe from the steering position. I wondered about the composition of such a meal on board such a ship, but my curiosity was soon assuaged when a bluejacket appeared bearing three steaming mugs of sweetened cocoa and some hard ship's biscuit.

"I recommend softening it in the cocoa first," Captain Glover smiled to me, following his own advice as I gingerly approached the second item on the menu. Though I have broken my fast more luxuriously on many occasions, that simple food and drink taken as we watched the sun rise over the Solent remains as one of the more memorable meals of my life. Holmes devoured his repast while continuing to scan the horizon.

Captain Glover leaned towards me and spoke in a low voice. "Is it your opinion that your friend has a solution to the mystery?"

"I believe he does," I answered in the same quiet tone. "But I have no idea what the solution might be, or how he might have arrived at it."

We continued on our way, with the inlet to Southampton harbour clearly visible. Our ship was, so Captain Glover assured me, in a perfect position to observe all the comings and goings of the port, and indeed we saw many different kinds of craft, from the largest ocean liners setting sail for distant parts of the Empire, to smaller fishing and pleasure craft. Several times we spotted approaching steamers that appeared to match the description with which we had been provided, but none of them proved to be the vessel we sought.

At length, Fanshawe called excitedly, "We have her!" and raced along the deck to join us, passing his binoculars to Captain Glover, who passed them in his turn to Holmes.

"Well done, Mr Fanshawe," exclaimed Glover. "Intercept her course as you think best. I shall stay well out of your way in this matter."

"Aye, aye. Thank you, sir," replied the Lieutenant, and we heard a series of nautical orders being issued, most of them totally incomprehensible to my ears.

It was not long, though, before it was obvious that we were on a course where we would cross the path of the *Matilda Briggs* in a relatively short time.

"Man the gun, Mr Fanshawe," bellowed Captain Glover. "We may need to fire a shot across her bow."

"Aye, aye, sir," and a group of sailors took their position by the 12-pounder. My heart was racing as this marine chase drew to a close, and Holmes, I noticed, was white-lipped and tense while we closed in on the coaster. We were now close enough to see the name written on the bow without the aid of a telescope or binoculars.

"Make the signal 'I D', Mr Fanshawe."

"Aye, aye, sir." Two flags went up the mast and fluttered at the head.

"What is the meaning of that signal, Captain?" I asked.

"'Heave to or I will fire into you'," he replied.

Holmes heard this exchange and whirled around to face us. "We must not fire into her!" he exclaimed. We cannot risk injury to the passenger we believe may be on board."

"Have no fear, Mr Holmes," answered Glover. "We will do no such thing."

The *Matilda Briggs* showed no sign of stopping or even of slowing. "Damn their eyes!" shouted Glover, angrily. "One over the bow, if you please, Mr Fanshawe."

The sailors manning the bow gun went through complex well-drilled motions, culminating in a deafening explosion that made my ears ring, with a bright flash and a cloud of smoke issuing from the muzzle of the gun. A few seconds later, a column of water arose some fifty yards ahead of the *Matilda Briggs*.

"Good shooting," commented Glover. The shell appeared to have the desired effect, and the froth of water at the stern of the other ship died away and the *Matilda Briggs* visibly slowed in the water.

"Bring us alongside, Mr Fanshawe," ordered Captain Glover, and within a few minutes, we were beside the rusty plates of the other's hull.

"We will board her," announced Glover.

"Very good, sir," replied Fanshawe. "I will assemble a boarding party."

"You will do no such thing," retorted the Captain. "By 'we', I mean Mr Holmes, Dr Watson and myself only. There are to be no others. However, if we have not returned or otherwise indicated our safety to you within fifteen minutes of boarding, you may lead a boarding party at your discretion. I have my pistol. Are you two gentlemen armed?" turning to Holmes and myself. "I feel it would be a wise precaution here."

"We are not," replied Holmes. "I would prefer not to carry a weapon, but if you feel it would be necessary, I will abide by your decision."

"Mr Fanshawe, you will provide these gentlemen with pistols," Glover ordered *Daring*'s skipper.

We were duly provided with heavy Navy revolvers, and

Fanshawe hailed the *Matilda Briggs*, expressing the intention of boarding. A ladder was dropped from her deck, and we scrambled up it, Captain Glover leading, Holmes following, and myself bringing up the rear.

Once on board, I looked around. As had been reported, the crew were Asiatics of some description – I assumed from the Dutch East Indies. A savage-looking people, they regarded their visitors with sullen stares. Though none seemed armed, there are enough potential weapons on board a ship of the type of the *Matilda Briggs*, such as marlinspikes and other nautical implements, to give me pause for thought.

"Where is your Captain?" roared Glover at the closest native, who seemed to be in charge of the others. His only answer was a blank stare, in which incomprehension and hostility appeared to be mixed.

"*Waar is uw kapitein?*" he asked. This brought a response from the crewman, who passed an order to one of the others, using a language that was totally unfamiliar to me.

After a minute or so, a tall European, about fifty years old by his appearance, and with a skin that had, to my experienced eye, seen many a tropic day, emerged from the bridge and joined us on deck.

"Gerard Waalfort, master of the *Matilda Briggs*," he introduced himself in English that was hardly accented. "Is there any way I can assist you gentlemen? I hope you are aware that your shell has disturbed my crew, and I trust you have a good reason for your actions."

"Indeed we have," replied Holmes, stepping forward. "We are looking for Lord Haughton, whom we have reason to believe is aboard this vessel."

"An English lord?" scoffed the other. "Does this rusting bundle of steel plates look like a luxury passenger liner to you? The kind of vessel on which an English lord would travel?" He threw back his head and laughed.

"Maybe you know your passenger better as Augustus Wilmott?" suggested Holmes quietly.

The laughter choked off abruptly. "He is a lord?" asked Waalfort. "You are not joking?" Holmes shook his head. "*Mijn God!*" exclaimed the Dutchman.

"Ramsay-Moffat did not inform you?" asked Holmes, smiling gently. By my side, Captain Glover stiffened at Holmes' mention of the name of his subordinate, and seemed about to speak, but I plucked him by the sleeve, and motioned to him to hold his peace. To his credit, he did so, though I could see he was more than anxious to ask questions of Holmes.

"He said nothing," replied the Dutch skipper, before realising what he had admitted. "*Mijn God!*" he repeated. "Are you some kind of wizard to know these things?"

"I think you had better lead us to Lord Haughton," Holmes said in reply.

"Very good, Mr Wizard," was the answer. He led the way down a companionway to a dark and noxious hold in the bowels of the ship. "Here," gesturing towards one corner.

A pitiful sight met our eyes. A gaunt ragged figure, clad in rags and lying on the deck of the hold, stared up at us, and a flicker of recognition dawned in his eyes.

"My God, it's Glover!" croaked the scarecrow.

"In the name of all that's damnable," said the Captain, seemingly aghast. "Lord Haughton!"

"Come no closer," replied the other. "I am dying. Come closer to me, and it is your death, too."

"I am a doctor," I informed him. "I can assist you."

"No, do not come near!" he answered me. "It is certain death for you to approach. I know not what it is that ails me, but suspect the worst, and I am convinced it is deadly."

Despite myself, I shrank a little, but moved to fulfil the duties of my profession. Sadly, it took less than a minute for me to make my diagnosis. "It is the plague, the Black Death," I announced to the others. Holmes and Captain Glover instinctively moved back several paces, but I held my ground.

The dying man looked at me with the calm eyes of those who know their fate, and are resigned to it. "I am sorry, Doctor, to have placed you in such danger."

"I am not afraid," I said. In truth, I was naturally more than a little concerned, but less so than others would be under the circumstances, as a result of my previous exposure to the foul disease during an epidemic that had broken out in my time in India. This experience afforded me, I fervently hoped, some immunity. "Some clean water," I ordered the Dutchman. "And blankets."

I bent over the sick man, and discovered that, in my opinion, based on my previous Indian experience, he had not exaggerated his condition. He had, in my estimation, only a few hours, possibly even less, before his death. The water arrived, Waalfort passed it at arm's length to me, and I held it to the dying man's lips. He drank of it thirstily, and fell to coughing.

"I must inform *Daring* that we are safe – for the moment," said Glover. He left us, escorted back to the deck by Waalfort, and Holmes and I were left alone with the sick man.

"How did you contract the disease?" I asked him. "Are some of the crew of this ship suffering?"

For answer, he waved his hand feebly towards another corner of the hold. Holmes moved to see what it was to which he had gesticulated, and I heard his cry of surprise.

"What is it, Holmes?" I called to him.

"Some animals," he replied. "They resemble rats, but they are larger than any I have hitherto encountered. Hideous creatures the size of terriers."

"They are indeed rats," gasped Haughton. "The giant rat of Sumatra, brought from the East Indies, and a known carrier of disease. There are many of them on this boat. When I was brought on board, I was placed next to the filthy animals, and…" He fell to coughing, vomiting up a sticky mess, and for several minutes was unable to speak, while I mopped his brow with a wet cloth, and provided such comfort as I was able. "I am going," were his next words, as I raised the water to his mouth once more. "I thank you for your kindness, and—" his words ceased.

I examined him as closely as I dared. "He is dead, Holmes."

"So quickly?"

"It is a malady that strikes quickly and without notice, and the final stages are mercifully swift," I told him. "May he rest in peace," I added as I closed his eyes, "whatever wrongs he may have done in his life."

We mounted to the upper deck, thankful to be out of the foul air of the hold, and informed Captain Glover of the situation.

"This ship must not land under any circumstances," said Glover. "The danger of the plague spreading to England is too great. Hoist 'V B' – 'sickness is contagious' as soon as possible," he ordered Waalfort, who hastened to obey. The crew, for their part, seemed demoralised, and their previous sullen, almost aggressive, nature seemed to have turned to a silent resentment.

Glover then demanded a megaphone and called to the waiting skipper of *Daring*, "The crew of this ship must enter quarantine immediately. Order a suitable ship to bring them off, and then return here. Make sure you have live torpedoes on board and an adequate supply of shells for the gun."

"You cannot sink my ship!" exclaimed the Dutchman, aghast as he perceived Glover's intentions.

"I can and I will. Your ship is a danger to my country," replied the Englishman imperturbably. "Mynheer Waalfort, I want to point out that you yourself are in grave danger, together with all your crew, of spending the rest of your life in an English prison. If you prefer, I can arrange for your ship to be sunk with all of you on board, and you can take your chances in the water? No? Then I suggest that you accept the course of action I suggest."

"We are many and you are but three," pointed out the other, snarling.

"I feared it might come to this," Holmes interrupted. "Before you start considering that kind of action, you might wish to take one or two other points into consideration."

"Such as?"

"First, the fact that it is known we are on board this ship. Were we to be missing when the *Daring* returns, I would venture to suggest that you would not even reach jail, but you and your crew would not even reach dry land."

"That may well be true, but I am prepared to take that chance. Anything else?"

"The most persuasive argument I can make," said Holmes, "is the revolver that Watson here has pointed at your head."

While the last conversation had been taking place, I had crept to one side and pulled the Navy pistol from my pocket, cocking the hammer, and aiming it, unseen by my target, at the skipper. He turned and blanched.

"A convincing argument, I admit."

"And if you wish to consider two further arguments, I am holding one," producing his own revolver, "and Captain Glover has another." The coaster's skipper nodded silently.

"Now order your men to the rail, to sit facing the ocean, with their legs over the side of the ship," said Holmes. When that had been done, he asked, "We have twelve men here. How many are below?"

"Five stokers and engineers. And there are two officers off-watch."

"I will bring them up here," volunteered Captain Glover. He ducked into the companionway, and returned a few minutes later driving five more Asiatics before him at the point of his pistol. "And now for the officers." This time he entered the superstructure below the bridge, and almost immediately, we heard the cracks of two pistol shots. After a short while, a white man, clad in pyjamas, came on deck, his hands in the air, followed by our brave Captain.

"Where is Jan, the mate?" asked Waalfort.

"He tried to kill me," replied Glover, laconically. "He failed to do so, as you can see. I am here, and he is not."

The Dutch officer was forced to the side of the ship, where he sat alongside the crew, his legs dangling over the side.

"Can we count on your good behaviour now?" Holmes asked Waalfort. "Or do we ask you to join the crew?"

"I will stay here," replied the other, truculently.

"Dr Watson, keep your eye on him," ordered Glover. "Have no hesitation in firing should he attempt any tricks." The Dutchman stood motionless, his arms folded in front of him.

"What is that about Ramsay-Moffat?" asked Captain Glover to Holmes, in a low voice.

Holmes briefly outlined the story he had heard from the two *Colossus* officers, as Glover listened in mounting disbelief.

"You suspect my First Lieutenant of some sort of involvement in this affair?" he burst out at length.

"Waalfort here has already said as much."

"I confess that I have never regarded him highly as an officer on board my ship, and he held his position as First Lieutenant by reason of his seniority rather than his abilities," said Glover. "But for him to be involved in this kind of business... Words fail me." He bit his lips and stood brooding silently until the *Daring* returned.

IN AN hour's time, we were re-joined by the torpedo boat destroyer.

"Stand to windward," called out Glover. "Let us reduce the risk of infection if we can," he added to us.

"Are you and your crew not afraid of the disease you are carrying?" Holmes asked Waalfort, curiously.

"Not at all," he answered. "Or, to be more accurate, only a little. All of us have suffered from the plaag – the plague – in the past and lived to tell the tale. We are hardened to its effects, as I informed Captain Ramsay-Moffat when we discovered that the rats were carrying it."

"Excuse me," said Captain Glover. "Did I hear you say *Captain* Ramsay-Moffat?" His tone was quiet, but carried an air of menace about it.

"Why, yes. He is a Captain in the British Royal Navy, is he not?"

"He is no such damned thing, and never will be, if I have anything to do with it!" Captain Glover was fairly dancing with rage, and his face had turned an alarming shade of dark red.

"Calm yourself, Captain," urged Holmes. "There will be time enough for this later." He turned back to Waalfort. "Why were you carrying Lord Haughton on your ship? Was money your motive there?"

"We were told by Captain Ramsay—" He checked himself, observing a possible further explosion from Glover, and continued, "Ramsay-Moffat told us that we could expect money from this trip, yes, but this was done largely to protect myself. Years ago in Jakarta while I was serving in the Colonial Police, I committed an indiscretion – it was not a serious indiscretion, and I am by no means the only one to have committed such – but if it were brought to the attention of the authorities, even today, I would lose my pension, and I might even face prison, if proof could be brought against me. I believed that no such proof existed. Ramsay-Moffat, with whom I had been in contact since the days of Jakarta when he was stationed there told me that the man whom I had known in Jakarta as Augustus Wilmott was likely to be made a very important man in the government, and that even without proof, his word would count against mine, no matter what proofs of innocence I produced." He shrugged his shoulders. "And as I confess to you now, I am guilty of those past crimes. I could produce no such proofs."

"Much as I had surmised," said Holmes. "And the idea was to keep your prisoner on board until he agreed not to threaten you and Ramsay-Moffat in the future?" The other nodded. "And the rats? Did you know they carried the plague with them?"

"That, I swear, was not our intention. Ramsay-Moffat

had told us that Wilmott had a fear of these rodents and that if we kept him below next to the cage in which they were confined, he would soon agree to our terms. But even when I cabled to Ramsay-Moffat that we suspected we had the plague on board, he would not listen to any change in our plans."

"And so, instead of agreeing to your demands, your prisoner contracted this foul disease, from which he has now died," pointed out Holmes. "I do not know how this is going to sit with an English jury."

"I do not know how Ramsay-Moffat is going to sit with me when I have finished with him," growled Captain Glover.

"Control yourself, Captain," Holmes implored him. "I am sure your feelings do you credit, but let us await the outcome of this episode before we do much else. But, mark!"

A white ship, a red cross pained on her side, was approaching the *Matilda Briggs*. "Your transport to shore, skipper," Holmes announced to Waalfort.

"Hah!" replied the Dutchman, and thrust his hands deep into his trouser pockets.

The hospital ship, the *Nightingale*, came alongside, and the crew of the *Matilda Briggs* were transferred to her, Captain Waalfort leaving his ship last in the traditional fashion.

"To the prison hospital with them," Captain Glover shouted to the *Nightingale*. "They must be closely guarded and kept away from others." He turned to us. "And what do we do? We are possibly infected, and I do not wish to be the cause of spreading the plague throughout the Fleet by contact with *Daring*'s crew."

"May I suggest that *Daring* lower her boat, and the three of us board her and move away from this vessel while *Daring* destroys her. We can then be towed back to Portsmouth, and the medical authorities can take whatever steps they see fit," I put forward.

"I concur," agreed Glover, after a short pause for thought. "What do we do with the body of poor Lord Haughton, though?"

"Let it be said that he went down with the ship," replied Holmes. "None of this business must reach the public's ears, as I am sure you understand."

"It is a Viking's funeral, I suppose. From all I hear of the man, it is an ending that he would have wished for himself."

The boat was lowered, and Glover and I rowed the boat away from the *Matilda Briggs*. "Ahoy!" he shouted to the *Daring* when he we were at a distance he estimated would be safe. "Fire at will, Mr Fanshawe," he called through the megaphone we had brought with us.

There was a muffled thumping sound, and a long cylinder seemed to leap from the bow of the *Daring*. "A Whitehead torpedo," explained Glover. "Two hundred pounds of guncotton should put paid to that hell-ship."

We watched the torpedo's trail, easily visible as a consequence of the escaping compressed air by which it was propelled, speeding towards its target. After less than a minute, the sea erupted at the waterline of the *Matilda Briggs*, and the sound of the explosion reached us a few seconds later. Almost immediately, the coaster heeled over, and in a matter of minutes, nothing remained on the surface other than a few wooden fragments, and an oily scum.

"Excellent work by Fanshawe," commented Glover, as we were towed back to port by *Daring* at the end of a long rope.

On arrival at the port, I explained our situation to the doctors who had charge of the *Matilda Briggs'* crew. Based on my report of the nature and length of our exposure, they recommended salt baths for the three of us, together with some unpleasant-tasting prophylactic medicines. Whether it was due to these precautions, or whether it was a matter of luck, I do not know, but we escaped infection.

"In many ways, one of the simplest cases I have encountered," Sherlock Holmes told Mycroft as we sat together in Baker Street. "I fail to see how you missed all the clues."

Mycroft had been persuaded by his brother to leave his familiar circuit of his lodgings, Whitehall and the Diogenes Club on account of the sensitive nature of the information that Holmes was about to impart to us. On arrival at Baker Street, he had sniffed superciliously at Holmes' eccentric domestic arrangements, but had at length allowed himself to be settled in an armchair with a brandy and soda by his side. Sherlock Holmes was now recounting the story to him and to me. On our return from Portsmouth, I had returned to my practice, and I had not seen

Holmes for two days while he clarified the answers to a few final problems regarding the case. Earlier that day, I had received a telegram from him, requesting my presence. I was keen to know the details, and I gladly accepted.

I was anxious to know of the fate that had befallen the players in this affair, and I asked Holmes if he had received any news thereon.

"I received a dispatch from the good Captain Glover yesterday," Holmes replied. "He managed to maintain control of his feelings sufficiently to confront Ramsay-Moffat without recourse to physical violence, and presented him with the evidence of his crimes. Given the choice between a court-martial, which might have passed a capital sentence and would undoubtedly have ruined him on the one hand, and the gentleman's recourse in these circumstances on the other, Ramsay-Moffat selected the latter. His body was discovered floating in Portsmouth harbour the same evening, a bullet-hole through the right side of the head. A letter addressed to Captain Glover was discovered in his cabin."

"A most unpleasant business, even for a blackmailer, would you not say?"

"Most unpleasant," repeated Sherlock Holmes, "in that we had two blackmailers, blackmailing each other. Haughton and Ramsay-Moffat were linked by a cord of mutual distrust and hatred."

"One would have assumed that the two would cancel each other out," I said. "Where both are blackmailers, surely there is nothing to expose."

"Nothing and everything," replied Holmes. "For

Lord Haughton, the exposure of his escapade in Jakarta all those years ago would almost certainly lead to the complete collapse of his career. On the other hand, we now know, thanks to the confession he left behind, that Ramsey-Moffat's own promotions were largely due to an admixture of the influence wielded at his behest by his victim, Haughton, and by his destruction of the careers of other officers through bullying and blackmail over minor peccadilloes, as well as outright forgery of orders and documents in a number of cases. Naturally, Haughton was aware of all this, and had it in his power to wreck Ramsay-Moffat in his turn. He was, strange though it may seem, in a stronger position than the other. If he were to expose Ramsay-Moffat, the latter would have nothing on which to fall back, while Haughton, of course, would have his estates and eventually his father's title. The two were like fencers with their foils at each other's throats, neither daring to move forward for fear of the damage they might inflict on themselves."

"How did you come to know that Ramsay-Moffat was involved, Sherlock?" asked his brother, speaking for the first time.

"From the letters written by Haughton," replied Holmes, bringing out the copies that had been supplied by Mycroft.

"I examined these letters and could make nothing of them," exclaimed Mycroft. "Perhaps you would be good enough to explain yourself here."

"It was not until after we had been introduced to Ramsey-Moffat that the meaning became clear," explained Holmes. Read the first letters of each epistle."

"'Read' – R." Mycroft turned to the next sheet. "'As' – A, and the next starts 'My' – M, and the next is 'Some' – S. R A M S… I see it now. Ingenious."

"Too ingenious," replied my friend. "You missed it entirely, and it was too late for me to act on it when I had discovered its meaning. However, it was obvious to me that there was more to these letters than met the eye. The letters were written at Waalfort's orders, I am sure, in order to allay any fears that Haughton was dead, and the captive developed a plan, too subtle for its own good, to communicate with the outside world. The whole message, by the way, read 'R A M S A Y M O F F A T A S K H I M W H E R E I A M'. Following Lord Haughton's contracting the plague, the communications naturally ceased. My suspicions regarding Ramsay-Moffat were aroused, you will remember, Watson, when he told us the whole of the story regarding the past incident in Jakarta – you do not need to know the details, Mycroft. It was a sordid little tale that reflects well on no-one and is best forgotten, but it was indicative of some kind of devilment on Ramsay-Moffat's part. Following his tale to us, I re-examined the letters."

"And that was enough to put you on the track of the *Matilda Briggs*?"

"The connection was obvious. My enquiries at the docks confirmed that there was a link with the East Indies in the shape of the crew and the officers. We knew that both Haughton and Ramsey-Moffat had served in that part of the world, and it therefore seemed more than likely that Ramsey-Moffat had retained connections there. Waalfort turns out to have been one of the police officials who brought Haughton back to the *Bellorophon* that fateful night. He admitted to us that he had committed misdeeds – maybe he accepted bribes, or worse – and somehow Haughton had discovered this. I have no doubt that Ramsay-Moffat also had this knowledge, and used it to further his own ends.

"After that, it was plain that there was some form of blackmail afoot. Ramsay-Moffat had been using his knowledge of Haughton's past to further his own career, but dared not push too hard, for fear he himself would be exposed. It has transpired that many documents in his Service file are not authentic, and he would most certainly have suffered had their authenticity been questioned."

"What caused him to adopt these desperate measures at the last?" asked Mycroft.

"I believe it was exactly as we were told by Waalfort," replied Holmes. "Haughton was believed to be on his way to greater things – even if your championing of him as First Lord of the Admiralty was not common knowledge, Mycroft, it seems that he was highly regarded by many. His word would have carried much more weight than previously, and any attempt by Ramsey-Moffat to use his knowledge against his superior would be dismissed as the ravings of a failed rival."

"You appear to have saved the country from two plagues, Sherlock. Not only a physical disease, but also a moral plague that could have infected our political system. Your bravery in confronting this threat is commendable."

"You should rather be commending Watson for his bravery," commented my friend. "To approach and give comfort to a man you know is dying of such a vile disease argues a degree of courage that few possess. I frankly confess, Watson, I am humbled by your actions."

I was embarrassed, and muttered something about its only having been my duty.

"Nonetheless," said Mycroft, "I concur with Sherlock in his opinion."

Naturally, none of the above was ever made public, nor do I intend it to be so, given the high positions held by some of the principals of the case, and the importance of them to the Crown. Lord Haughton was given out as having been lost at sea in a boating accident, and the capsized wreck of his yacht was adduced as proof of this.

Captain Glover, I am pleased to say, remained firm friends with Holmes and myself for many years to come, and largely as a result of Mycroft Holmes' invisible influence, rose to the rank of Rear-Admiral, a promotion, in my opinion, well deserved. Waalfort and his crew were held in quarantine, after which time a request was made to the Dutch government, and they were returned to Holland on a Dutch naval vessel. I never discovered their ultimate fate.

Holmes, as was his wont, refused all honours and glory connected with the business, and I followed his lead on this matter, though I have sometimes wondered how my and Mary's lives would have been changed had I yielded to the momentary impulse, and we had henceforth been addressed as Sir John and Lady Watson.

About the Author

Hugh Ashton came from the UK to Japan in 1988 to work as a technical writer, and has remained in the country ever since.

When he can find time, one of his main loves is writing fiction, which he has been doing since he was about eight years old.

As a long-time admirer of Sir Arthur Conan Doyle's famous detective, Sherlock Holmes, Hugh has often wanted to complete the canon of the stories by writing the stories which are tantalizingly mentioned in passing by Watson, but never published. This latest offering of three such stories brings Sherlock Holmes to life again.

More Sherlock Holmes stories from the same source are definitely on the cards, as Hugh continues to recreate 221B Baker Street from the relatively exotic location of Kamakura, Japan, a little south of Tokyo.

If you enjoyed this book, look for Hugh's other books:
Tales From the Deed Box of John H. Watson MD
Beneath Gray Skies
At the Sharpe End
Red Wheels Turning and
Keiko's House
All available at Smashwords.com and other fine booksellers.

If you have questions or constructive comments, feel free to contact Hugh at HAshton@inknbeans.com

Made in the USA
Lexington, KY
11 August 2012